INVINCIBLE

.

INVINCIBLE

Book One of the Legends of Legacy Fleet
Series

David Bruns

www.nickwebbwrites.com

Summary: The aliens took her ship. Commander Halsey wants it back. For decades they were among us, silently infiltrating the power structures of society. Now the Swarm stands on Earth's doorstep. As humanity launches a desperate counter-attack, the alien victory seems inevitable. For Halsey, this is personal. While the Fleet executes their battle plan, she leads a do-or-die suicide strike at the heart of the alien force: her own Invincible, turned into a weapon against mankind. With time running out Halsey fights to take back her command and save the human race--or die trying. She is a proud warrior. She is humanity's last hope. She is Invincible.

Text set in Garamond

Designed by Nick Webb

Cover art by Tom Edwards

http://tomedwardsdmuga.blogspot.co.uk

ISBN: 9781798985250

Printed in the United States of America

Chapter 1

Missionary ship SS *Galilee*
Uncharted territory, 126 light-years from United Earth
Space

There was no easy way to come out of stasis. The training vids said it got easier each time, but this was her fourth rotation awake and *nothing* was easier.

Sister Elaine Cornwell peeled the patches off her eyes and carefully disconnected the shunt in her carotid artery. The wake-up drugs were already kicking in, allowing her to stand on wobbly knees. She grimaced as she stripped off the bodysuit that both monitored her vitals and stimulated her muscles while she was in stasis. The sensors were held together by a loose mesh that left an imprint on her skin like she'd been wrapped up in chicken wire for the last three years.

That was their rotation: thirty days awake every three years, thirty days being the average time a human could live alone and not go bonkers. The towel was rough against her skin, but it felt good to *feel* something again. That was the other thing they never told you about stasis. She'd been asleep for twelve years now and couldn't remember feeling a gosh-darned thing.

A red light blinked on the panel in front of her. She stopped rubbing the towel and focused on the words. Bless the Lord, her mind was like oatmeal—another side effect of stasis, thank you very much.

Emergency Wake-Up Protocol. T minus 5.

Elaine cleared her throat. "Moses, why did you wake me five days early?"

Moses, the ship's computer, responded, "Good morning, Sister Cornwell. You were withdrawn from stasis five days early because the ship is currently operating in an unmanned status. That is against protocol."

Elaine racked her brain. Who was before her in the staffing rotation? Brother Michael.

"Moses, where is Brother Michael?"

"Brother Michael is no longer on the ship."

Alarmed and exasperated at the same time, Elaine yanked a plain brown jumpsuit out of the locker and started to pull it on. "Moses, where was Brother Michael last seen?"

"Brother Michael was last seen at Airlock Six."

Elaine did her best to walk fast, but she had to stop to catch her breath twice. The stasis suit did a fine job keeping her muscles toned, but cardio was another story. She hawked up a gob of something crusty and spat it onto the deck.

Airlock Six was on the maintenance deck in the belly of the ship. She hadn't been in this area since before they'd left Mars Station. Elaine instructed Moses to turn on the lights as she entered the deck, but the harsh illumination left plenty of shadows among the parked equipment.

"Hello? Brother Michael?" Her voice sounded thin, pitiful in the huge space.

She kept to the center aisle; the only sound in the vast bay was her bare feet slapping against the deck. She should have worn shoes; her feet were still tender from the stasis fluid. Airlock Six was all the way at the back of the bay, behind some kind of huge yellow tractor. What was Michael doing down here?

Finally, she reached the airlock, but there was no sign of her crewmate. Elaine stood on her tiptoes to peer into the dark airlock. Nothing. She fumbled at the operator's panel to turn on the lights and got back up on her toes.

Her scream echoed in the vast open bay.

Brother Michael's body floated in the airlock, anchored by a short tether to one of the metal stanchions in the center of the space. Elaine sank to the unyielding metal deck and screamed until her voice was nothing but a harsh whisper. She hugged her knees and said a prayer—anything she could remember—over and over again.

She hugged and rocked and whimpered until the thought finally penetrated her mind: she was the only person awake on the entire ship. If anything was going to get done, she was going to have to do it.

Elaine dragged herself back to the panel. She kept blinking. Her tear ducts were still clogged with stasis fluid and her eyeballs felt like they might burst from the pressure. Moses didn't operate by voice down here and she had to consult the instructions twice to get the lock repressurized and artificial gravity restored. The airlock doors made a hideous grinding clang as they opened.

She tried not to look at Michael's face, but it was impossible not to. She'd seen pictures of what rapid depressurization did to the human body, but seeing it in person was worse, far worse. Michael's dark skin was stretched tight across his features like leather and all the blood vessels in his eyes had burst, leaving him with a devilish stare. His tongue, a dried lump of flesh, protruded from his mouth.

He was tied to the stanchion in the center of the airlock by a meter-long tether, his body rigid, one hand reaching up.

"Oh, Michael, what have you done?" Elaine whispered, her voice echoing in the airlock. The tear duct in her right eye suddenly cleared and tears began streaming down half her face. She dragged him the five meters out of the airlock, wincing at the sound of his dry flesh scraping the floor, then went through the procedure to shut the massive doors.

She covered Michael's body with a tarp she scavenged from one of the machines in the bay, promising herself she'd give him a proper burial later.

Elaine looked at the body, then at the airlock. Her brain felt like it was still stuck in low gear. There was something wrong about this, but she couldn't quite put her finger on it.

Never mind. Right now her main priority was the safety of the *Galilee* and her sleeping crew.

She stopped by her locker on her way to the bridge and put her boots on. The soft material felt wonderful on her bruised feet. She also snatched a handful of protein bars from the galley. Still chewing, Elaine entered the bridge and scanned the flight data. All fine. She keyed in her approval code for the next twenty-four hours of flight.

She sank into the command chair, allowing the cushions to conform to her frame. She was so tired even eating was an effort. The sprint to the maintenance deck, the shock of

4

finding Michael's body, the long trek back to the bridge . . . her eyelids drooped, and all she wanted to do was curl up and take a nap.

No. She sat up in the chair by sheer force of will.

"Moses, show me the activity logs for the last three days."

The data spooled down the screen. It was line after line of routine adjustments, mostly done by Moses with approvals from Michael where required. She stopped the feed, using her eyescan to highlight a line of text.

Access to Embryo Storage Locker 3D.

In addition to the three dozen crew in stasis, the *Galilee* carried embryos for all sorts of creatures, including humans. They liked to think of themselves as a modern-day Noah's ark. Locker 3D was for humans. Why in Heaven's name would Michael access human embryo storage?

Elaine was back on her feet now, running again. She called out as she entered the science lab, "Moses, open Embryo Storage Locker Three Delta. Access code Cornwell, Elaine, seven-six-bravo-three."

"Access code confirmed. Opening Storage Locker Three Delta."

Elaine held up her arms as she passed through the biocontainment airlock. She slipped a facemask over her nose and mouth as she entered the secure area and made her way down the row.

The locker was standing open when she arrived. The third shelf was empty.

Elaine forced herself to think. Each shelf held one hundred embryos. Michael had removed one hundred human embryos from storage. Why?

5

"Moses, close Locker Three Delta." The heavy metal door slid shut with a sigh.

Back on the bridge, Elaine called up the activity logs again. She started reading from where she'd left off at the embryo access entry. Halfway down the next screen she stopped, reread a line, and sat back in her chair.

Ship's database. Complete download.

Michael had taken a hundred human embryos and then downloaded a complete copy of the *Galilee*'s database. Why?

The prickle of an idea, that thing she had missed earlier, worried her mind again. Elaine closed her eyes and went through everything that had happened to her since she'd been woken up. She forced herself to slow down, remember every detail, every sensation.

Waking up . . . the red light . . . the frantic trip to the airlock . . . fumbling with the airlock controls . . . unhooking Michael's corpse. Her eyes snapped open. That was it. The maintenance airlock had been vented, but from where Michael had been tethered in the center of the large airlock, there was no way he could have reached the controls to shut the outer door.

Elaine started to shake.

Someone else had been on the ship.

Chapter 2

Forty years later

ISS *Deliver*
On border patrol ten light-years outside United Earth space

Petty Officer Jon Olson stretched in his chair, stifling a yawn. Ninety more minutes, that's all that was left in his watch, just another fifty-four hundred seconds.

"Helm, come to course three-seven-zero, mark five."

Cripes, even Lieutenant Hurley sounded bored, Olson thought. Did anyone really think the Russians or the Chinese would try something this far out of occupied space? There was no one out here. No. One. Except us.

"Commencing sensor sweep, sir," Olson said. Standard Fleet policy: come to a new heading, look for the bogeyman that was out there to get you.

The meta-space band jumped. More like hiccupped, actually. Odd. Olson zoomed in on the reading. The trace showed the normal scatter, then *bam*, a massive burst of quantum energy, like a cosmic burp. The meta-space long-range sensors probably needed recalibration.

Olson considered ignoring it. He could pretend he never saw it and let the next shift take care of the calibration. But . . . he was up for promotion to first-class petty officer next month, and a letter of recommendation from Lieutenant Hurley would be a really nice addition to his packet. Why not use this opportunity to reinforce to the lieutenant what a fine young sailor he really was?

He spun in his chair. "Sir?"

Lieutenant Hurley's head swiveled toward Olson. The man's nostrils flared and his eyes burned with an unnatural light. "Go ahead, Sensors."

Olson shifted in his seat under the officer's glare. *Dial the intensity back to eight, dude. We're on the backshift.* He plastered a professional smile on his face. "Request permission to take the long-range sensors offline for a calibration. I'm getting a strange quantum fluctuation in the meta-space band."

"Really?" Hurley cocked his head like a dog listening to a distant sound. "Permission granted, Petty Officer Olson. Take the long-range sensors offline for calibration."

"Aye-aye, sir." Olson spun in his chair, his fingers automatically stabbing the screen. The meta-space band on his display started pulsing with a square wave test pattern. He cracked his knuckles. He now had seventy-six—make that seventy-*five*—minutes until he was off duty. Minus thirty for the calibration and he might as well just call it a day and hit the showers now.

"Communications Officer, take the transmit array offline and run a calibration."

"Sir?" Ensign Kelly Brooks's ponytail swung a wide arc as

she spun to face the watch officer.

"You heard me, Ensign. Calibrate the transmit array. Now."

Brooks's face reddened. "Sir, we need the captain's permission to take comms offline."

Hurley's tone hardened and Olson imagine the officer had dialed his visual intensity level on Brooks up to eleven. "Thank you for reminding me of Fleet regulations, Ensign. I have the captain's verbal permission to perform the maintenance."

Olson huffed. Fat chance of that. Captain Donaldson never did anything without writing it down first. The man was like a human paperwork volcano.

Brooks—God bless that woman's persistence—tried again. "Sir, I—"

"Ensign!" Hurley chopped at the air with the flat of his hand. Brooks's mouth hung open. "Take the transmit array offline. Now."

Brooks swallowed. "Aye-aye, sir."

From the corner of his eye, Olson could see the big red X flashing on her screen. Ensign Brooks's back was ramrod straight in her chair and the back of her neck was pink. Olson was glad he wasn't her roommate after this shift. That gal had some steam to vent.

His workstation trembled as if someone had jostled it. Odd. He placed his palm flat on the side of the panel. The faintest trace of a vibration tickled his skin.

Olson stabbed at the screen, stopping the calibration. "Sir," he said, sitting up in his chair, "I've got a physical vibration or something in the hull. Bringing the sensors back online."

"Leave them off, Olson." Hurley's voice was languid, not

like his normal clipped tones.

"Say again, sir?" Olson replied.

"I said leave them off." Hurley had a faraway look in his eye as if listening to distant music. He smiled.

Olson could feel the vibration in the soles of his feet now. He went through the final steps to bring the sensors back online and then just gaped at the screen. All the readings were off-scale high, as if every instrument was screaming at him.

"Sir! I don't understand these readings. There's something out there!" Olson could hear his voice climbing through the octaves, but he didn't care. He could feel the humming sound all around him now, as if it had infected their very atmosphere. "Putting it on screen."

Whatever it was, it wasn't Russian or Chinese or even Caliphate. His sensors were pegged high, completely useless as a source of data. Olson gaped. They were huge, bigger than a *Constitution*-class carrier even. He turned to look at the watch officer for orders.

Lieutenant Hurley was standing now, his arms spread wide, with a smile of pure ecstasy on his lips. His head lolled back as if he was drunk.

The lift door behind Hurley opened and Captain Donaldson strode onto the bridge. His gray hair was askew and he wore a plain white T-shirt with his uniform trousers. He stopped when he saw the screen, and Olson saw his face go slack with shock.

But the Old Man recovered quickly. Donaldson took one look at Hurley, then started shouting at Ensign Brooks. Olson could barely hear him over the droning sound that permeated the bridge.

"Message to Fleet CENTCOM—" He saw the big red X flashing on the comms panel and the color drained from his face. He whirled on Hurley. "What have you done?" he screamed.

Olson looked back at the screen. The alien ships were so close that the computer had readjusted the magnification. A flicker of green lightning lanced out of the lead vessel.

Chapter 3

ISS *Invincible*

On the border of Yalta Sector (Russian-controlled space)

"No!" Captain Jason Baltasar's roar made the very air of the bridge quiver. Executive Officer Addison Halsey gritted her teeth.

"Ensign Proctor, late again!" the captain continued. "How can we shoot something if we have no sensor inputs to fire control?"

He launched his six-foot-three frame out of the command chair and paced in front of the bridge crew. "We are here to *impress* the Russians, to scare them with our battle precision. You all understand this, right?" He waited until he saw nods all around. "Good." He leveled his stare at Halsey. "XO, secure from general quarters and let's run the drill again."

"Aye-aye, sir," Addison replied.

"I'll be in my ready room, Commander. Call me when you've got this lot sorted out." With a final disgusted glance, he strode away. Addison glared at the closed door of the ready room.

And leave me to clean up your mess, sir. Addison took a deep breath. This is not how it was supposed to work. The CO was the strategy guy, the one who set policy; the XO—her—was the tip of the spear, the one who executed that policy. She was the bad cop; he was the good cop.

Not with Baltasar. Addison had met micromanagers in her career, but this guy was a *nano*manager. He was into every detail, scarcely giving her time to breathe, much less do her friggin' job.

You don't choose your captain, your captain chooses you. She could almost hear her grandfather's voice in her head. The Old Man had done forty years in the Fleet, retiring as an admiral. Her family name went all the way back to World War Two on Earth, when the Fleet was a collection of steel ships sailing the oceans. She sighed to herself. Oh, for simpler times.

"Alright, people, you heard the captain. We're going to set up and run it again. This time we're going to break the fleet record for spot-to-shot," she said, referring to the drill that required them to sense, classify, and place at least one mag-rail round on an incoming hostile. The Fleet record was twelve seconds. They were at fifteen seconds and Captain Baltasar wanted his crew at ten.

"XO, the record is impossible," said the comms officer, Lieutenant Anders. "That was set years ago by the *Constitution*, under ideal conditions on a premeasured course. Why are we still doing this?"

Addison fixed Anders with a withering glare. "We are doing this, Lieutenant, because here on the *Invincible*, we don't chase records, we set the performance standard." She worked herself up so her voice carried to all the watch standers. "Is that clear, Anders?"

The comms officer swung back toward his station. "Yes, ma'am."

Anders was a good officer, he could take the heat. Proctor was another story. Addison strode to the sensors station and stood so her body was between Proctor and the rest of the bridge.

"How're you doing, Ensign?"

The poor kid was literally shaking from the bawling-out she'd gotten from the captain. She clenched her jaw and frowned at the screen. "Fine, ma'am."

"Zoe, look at me." She had the kind of deep green eyes that probably drove the male junior officers nuts, but the edges of her eyelids were quivering. *Christ, the kid is going to cry! When did I become a friggin' wet nurse? What kind of officers are the Academy graduating these days?*

Addison glanced over her shoulder. The rest of the bridge crew were all busy. She leaned over Proctor's station. "Here's the deal, Proctor. This drill is really all about you. Think about it: we've got twelve seconds to go from first contact to weapons away. If you take more than half of that time to classify the target and get coordinates over to fire control, we're dead. Got it?" Proctor nodded. Addison dropped her voice further. "This used to be my watch station, and there's a trick to cutting your time." Proctor was frowning now, listening intently, all trace of her previous frustration gone. *Maybe I misjudged her; this one's got grit.*

"What is it, XO? What's the trick?"

Addison called up a simulation on the screen. "Don't do double identification. Get one look, send it to fire control, *then* do your second look." She punched in the sequence while Proctor watched.

"But don't procedures require two looks?"

Addison nodded. "They do, but they don't specify the order. It's a loophole, but it's real. Besides, this is a hot war scenario, us against the Russkies. If that was really going down, we'd be firing on one look. Trust me." She smiled. "Besides, I happen to know the sensors officer on the *Constitution* and she told me that's how they got the record. Between you and me, there may have been alcohol involved."

"I can do that," Proctor said, nodding. "Thank you so much, XO."

"Don't thank me, Ensign. I'm just doing my job." She spun on her heel and raised her voice. "Alright, people, are we ready to kick some Russian ass this time?" Technically, the drill was against an unknown strike force, but everyone knew this was really a drill that simulated an attack by the Russians. Occasionally, the computer would throw in the Chinese or a friendly for good measure, but almost all the drones were programmed with Russian tactics.

Addison listened to affirmations from every bridge station, ending with Proctor on sensors: "Ready, ma'am." The ensign's back was straight, her chin set. Yes, Addison decided, I underestimated that one.

She marched to the door of the captain's ready room and punched the call button.

"Come," he said as he released the door.

Captain Baltasar stood with his broad back to the door, staring out the floor-to-ceiling windows at the emptiness of space.

"I'm disappointed, XO."

"Sir, I—"

Baltasar whirled on her. "Stop. I don't do excuses, Commander Halsey. I do results. You've been with me for nearly six months now and I would have figured a smart young officer like yourself would have taken that fact on board by now."

Addison bit the inside of her cheek, barely able to restrain herself from responding. They'd come out of space dock four weeks ago with half the crew new and he was dressing her down like some friggin' newbie greenhorn?

"When I requested you as my XO, I wanted the best—I expected the best." He was behind her now and he leaned close to her ear. "This is not your best, Commander."

She could feel the muscles of her jaw quivering, aching to be released, but she clamped her teeth together. Baltasar moved into her field of view, his icy blue eyes locking with hers. She met his gaze and held it. Seconds ticked away.

"Are you pissed off, Commander Halsey?"

She unclenched her jaw. "Yes, sir," she choked out, her eyes still fixed on his.

"Good. Let's go shoot some bad guys." He stalked out of the room. Addison followed.

Captain Baltasar swung into his command chair and ran a hand across his iron-gray crewcut. "Weapons Officer, release the drone."

Addison took her place behind the CO's chair. Now they waited. The drone would travel on a preset path, then reapproach the ship as a target. For the spot-to-shot drill, the clock started when sensors picked up the target.

Fifteen minutes later, Addison heard the sensors chirp and Proctor raised her voice. "Captain, sensors show an unidentified incoming vessel."

"Very well, Ensign," the captain replied. "XO, take us to general quarters."

"Aye-aye, sir," Addison said. She keyed her display. "All hands, general quarters." Addison counted to herself.

One-Mississippi, two-Mississippi . . .

Proctor was hunched over her screen, her fingers dancing across the panel. *C'mon, Proctor,* Addison thought.

Seven-Mississippi . . .

Addison saw Proctor hit the send key on her panel.

Ten-Mississippi . . .

The weapons officer sang out, "Captain, I have a firing solution on the incoming target. Request permission to fire."

Twelve-Mississippi . . .

Addison wanted to scream at the back of Baltasar's head. "Fire, dammit!"

"Weapons hold," the captain said.

"Captain, I—" Addison began.

"Captain!" Proctor broke in. "New classification is friendly. It's a merchant, sir!"

Addison felt a flush of embarrassment creep up her neck. Baltasar had switched the drone pattern on her. How could she have fallen for that?

"Stand down," the captain said. He looked over his shoulder and beckoned Addison closer. She could smell his aftershave.

"XO, if you ever advise a junior officer to break procedures like that again, I'll have you court-martialed. Do I make myself clear?"

Her cheeks were on fire, but she met his gaze. "Yes, sir."

Chapter 4

SS *Renegade*
Five light-years outside Caliphate space

Captain Laz Scollard plucked at his lip as he stared at the screen. Asteroid 8576543B looked like any one of the millions of asteroids in this part of space, but it wasn't. This asteroid was worth five million credits to him and his crew.

"Scan again," he said.

"Laz, this is like the third time I've scanned," said Mimi, his first officer. "There's nothing out there."

"Scan. Again. All frequencies, all sectors, very, very carefully."

"Yes, Your Highness," she came back with an unhealthy dose of snark. Again he regretted sleeping with Mimi—or Me-me, as he liked to think of her—but space was a lonely, boring place without someone to share your bunk with.

He forced Mimi out of his thoughts. The deal was the thing, and this one smelled to high heaven. The only part of the deal that didn't smell bad was the price tag. Five million credits was the score of a career, enough to retire on even. He'd be a legend in the privateer community—not that that meant much to him.

It seemed simple enough: pick up a "package" out in no-man's-land and take it to predesignated coordinates in the demilitarized zone between Russian and Chinese space. Easy peasy. With his cloaking device, he could slip in and out of anybody's space undetected, but the deal contained the three words every smuggler hated—*cash on delivery*. To complete the transaction, they'd have to uncloak, and that meant risk. In his experience, no one paid five million credits for an easy job.

To make matters worse, he had no idea who the package was from or who it was going to. Not that he hadn't tried to find out, but all of his connections came back empty-handed. And so Lazarus Scollard III was here, about to risk everything on the biggest payout of his career.

"Scans are clean, Laz," said Mimi. "Can we please get on with it?" She laid her hand on his thigh and squeezed. "You're overthinking it, dude. It's five *million* credits—that's ten times our normal rate. We all agreed, remember?"

She was right, they all had agreed. But it was his ship. If they got picked up, it'd be his neck on the line.

"Put-up-or-shut-up time, Captain Scollard," Mimi taunted. "You blow this one and I'll never sleep with you again."

Mimi might be a bitch, but she was also right. He punched the intercom.

"Topper, Little Dick, you guys ready?" he said.

"Standing by, Skipper," came the replies made tinny by the microphones in their space suits.

"Let's do this by the numbers, people. I'll turn off the cloak, send the activation code, and get us as close to the package as I can. You guys scoot out and grab the package, then we re-cloak and skedaddle out of here. I'll leave you guys on an open channel, but let's keep the bullshitting to a minimum. Any questions?"

There were none.

Laz's heart was racing. Five million credits will do that to you.

"Dropping the cloak," he said. "Mimi, send the code."

He winced as the pulse of energy left the ship. They'd just announced their presence to anyone within a radius of a few hundred thousand kilometers. Immediately, a steady blip of signal came back to them.

Mimi smiled. "Come to mama, baby. I've got a lock on the signal, Laz."

"Moving in," Laz replied, nudging the controls to move the *Renegade* closer to the asteroid. "Put the image on screen, Mimi. High mag." He scrutinized the viewscreen. "There." He stabbed at a blinking light on the craggy rock surface. Laz nosed his ship even closer. "Alright, guys, go pick this thing up. And hurry."

A few seconds later, Topper sailed past the cockpit on a long line. He used hand thrusters to slow his progress as he got closer to the surface of the asteroid. The blinking light went off.

"I got it, Skipper. Not very big, though. I've seen Little Dick take dumps bigger than this thing." Laz could hear the rest of the crew laughing on the open line.

"Knock it off, all of you," he shouted. "Get your ass back inside and let's get the hell out of here."

"Sorry, Skip," Topper said. "Reel me in, Little Dick."

***

Topper was right. The package really wasn't very big at all. Laz estimated it was less than half a meter square and light enough for one man to lift in normal gravity.

The *Renegade* was under the cover of her cloak and on her way to the preset drop-off coordinates. Everyone had gathered in the galley to see what five million credits looked like.

The answer was not much.

The matte black exterior was smooth except for the protruding light they'd used to locate it on the asteroid. Laz rapped his knuckles on the material. It sounded hollow. He looked at Gizmo. "Can you open it?"

Gizmo dug a finger in one armpit as he walked around the table in a slow circle. He pushed his glasses up his nose with his free hand, nodding absently.

"Are you sure that's a good idea?" Mimi asked.

Laz resisted the urge to make a smart-ass response. "This is a COD job. Let's see what's inside."

Gizmo chuckled to himself, then reached out and twisted the light fixture that protruded from the case. The black cube separated into two halves.

Topper elbowed Little Dick in the ribs. "Told ya." The two men were meatheads, but they were Laz's meatheads, and he knew he could trust them in a firefight.

A silver rectangle with a handle, about the size and shape of an attaché case, rode on a magnetic cushion inside the cube. Laz plucked it out of its magnetic cradle and laid it on the table. He squatted down for a closer look. Up close, he could see faint lines running all around the outer edge. On either side of the handle were two black discs. Locks?

Gizmo squatted down next to him. Laz could see the remnants of breakfast in the engineer's beard. "Whaddaya think, Gizmo?"

"Somebody went to a lot of trouble, sir." Gizmo was the only one on the ship who called him "sir." Like himself, the engineer was a Fleet refugee, just another dishonorable discharge who'd turned to the dark side of the private sector for a living. Somewhere deep inside, the man still retained a shred of respect for Laz's position as captain of the ship.

"Can you open it?" Laz asked.

Gizmo tugged on his beard, dislodging some food particles. "Mebbe. If I have enough time."

Laz looked up at Mimi. "How long till we get to the drop point?"

Mimi shrugged. "Twelve hours, give or take. I still don't think this is a good idea."

"And I still don't recall asking you for your opinion." Laz turned back to Gizmo. "Give it a shot?"

Gizmo nodded, his eyes never leaving the case.

***

It took the engineer eleven hours and change to open the case. Laz had given up hope that Gizmo would get it done before they reached the coordinates, but the man surprised him again.

"I got it, Captain," Gizmo said over the intercom with a hint of pride in his voice.

The galley was crowded with all manner of electrical

equipment, tools, and other gear, but the table that held the silver case was bare except for an electronic keyboard.

"Are you gonna play us a song, Gizmo?" Topper said, snickering. Little Dick chuckled alongside him.

"Knock it off, guys," Laz said to them. "We're meeting our mystery buyer in thirty minutes. No time for bullshitting around." He turned to Gizmo. "Tell me what you got."

"Resonance crypto," the engineer said. "Never seen anything like it. Pure genius. The only reason why I noticed it at all was that I was playing music while I had the case hooked up to the scope and saw a tiny response. I musta played the same song fifty times before I figured out the right chord."

Laz checked his watch. "Much as I'd love to see the big buildup here, Gizmo, we're about out of time. Let's cut to the chase."

"Yes, sir," he replied, with a touch of regret. "The case responds to a ten-note chord. Watch." He spread his fingers across the keyboard. The resulting sound was a screech of discordant notes, but after a few seconds the top of the case moved. "Go ahead and open it," Gizmo said over the racket.

Laz lifted the lid of the silver case. Inside, nestled in foam pockets, were twelve glass tubes about the size of Laz's index finger, each filled with glowing green liquid. He lifted one and held it up to the light. The liquid seemed viscous, reminding him of sparkly algae.

"What is it?" Topper asked, looking over Laz's shoulder.

Laz shook his head. "No idea." The goo inside the tube seemed to be moving on its own. Whatever it was, it gave him the creeps.

"Maybe it's a biological weapon," Little Dick said.

"Captain?" It was Mimi on the intercom. If she was calling him *Captain*, it must be serious.

"Go ahead, Mimi."

"There's a ship at our rendezvous point."

Laz felt the muscles of his stomach contract. That bad feeling about this deal was still there, nagging him like postnasal drip.

"Who's our lucky buyer?" he asked, trying to keep his voice light.

"The Chinese."

"Military or civilian?"

"Oh, definitely military."

"I'll be right up." He spun to face the rest of the crew. "Gizmo, seal the case back up and all three of you take it to Airlock One." He looked at Topper and Little Dick. "Full weapons complement, but no shooting. Understand? We want our money and we want to be around to spend it."

All three nodded, suddenly solemn.

Gizmo nodded to the tube that Laz held. "What about that one, sir?"

Laz slipped the tube into his breast pocket.

"This is a COD job," he said. "Insurance."

Chapter 5

CSS *Yangtze*
On patrol in Chinese-controlled space

A chirp penetrated the dark of Captain Sun Xiao's cabin. For a moment, he thought maybe he'd dreamed it, then it came again, followed by a crisp "Bridge to Captain."

His comms officer's voice . . . what was Wei doing awake at this time of night?

Rolling out of bed, he padded across the carpet to the screen on the wall. He carefully angled the screen so that the caller could not see his bed. No need to start rumors.

He tapped the screen. "Captain here."

Lieutenant Commander Wei's bald head filled the screen. "Captain, incoming transmission from Party Headquarters. Eyes only for you, sir. Shall I send it to your room?"

Xiao shot a glance at the still form in his bed and shook his head. "I'll take it in my ready room in five minutes, Wei."

He dressed in the dark, knowing every inch of his cabin by feel. The room still smelled faintly of the incense he'd burned the previous evening. A good evening, he reflected. No, a very good evening.

Before he left, Xiao leaned over the woman, nuzzling the dark hair at the nape of her neck. "I have to go," he whispered. "You can let yourself out?"

The woman sat up. She knew his question was code for "You need to leave now." Captain Sun's after-hours habits followed a strict—and well-known—code among the female crew members of the *Yangtze*. But none of them cared. As the nephew of the Chinese premier and the youngest commanding officer in the Chinese Fleet, Captain Sun Xiao was a highly sought-after prize by any ambitious woman. The Sun name was akin to royalty in today's Chinese society.

"Will I see you tonight?" she asked, eyeing him coquettishly through a fringe of dark hair.

Xiao considered her for a long moment. He'd have his personal secretary check into her family's background. "Perhaps," he replied. "But duty calls." He left her with a short bow.

Wei had roused the regular bridge crew in anticipation of new orders. "Captain on the bridge!" he called as Xiao stepped from the lift.

"At ease, everyone," Xiao said without breaking stride. He shot a questioning look at Wei. The officer saluted and said, "The transmission is queued up in your ready room, sir."

Xiao nodded. Wei was a good officer—better than his current XO, in fact. He made a mental note to put in a recommendation for his promotion.

He slid behind his desk and composed himself before answering the incoming call. He was stunned to see his uncle, Chinese Premier Sun Wu, staring back at him. Xiao instantly regretted the time he had taken before answering the call.

"Uncle," he said, trying to keep the embarrassment out of his voice. "What a pleasant surprise."

"Pleasant would have been five minutes ago, Nephew."

Xiao bowed his head at the screen. "I apologize for my tardiness, Uncle. Security matters kept me from answering your call immediately."

Wu huffed, then waved his hand. "No matter. I have an assignment for you, an issue of global security."

Xiao sat up straighter. "I am yours to command, sir." He studied his uncle. As his mother had once told him, it was important to listen to what his Uncle Wu did *not* say when he spoke.

In truth, the square-jawed man on the other side of the transmission was a puzzle. An orphan by birth, Sun Wu had burst onto the Chinese political scene a mere decade ago, climbing the web of social, political, business, and military connections with a speed that could only be described as breathtaking. Wu's marriage to Xiao's aunt had been a move calculated to win him the premiership, which had also changed Xiao's life forever. Overnight, he went from a mid-ranking officer with modest skills and marginal political clout to captain of a *Shaolin*-class starship.

In this case, Uncle Wu was careful not to say this was Chinese State business, which meant it was a personal endeavor.

"I'm sending you coordinates," his uncle said.

Xiao studied the star map: a point in space midway between the Russian- and Chinese-controlled sectors, in the demilitarized zone.

"You will meet a ship there. Caliphate-registered, a

smuggler. He will give you a package. Bring that package to me."

Xiao raised his eyebrows. "You want me to bring it back to Earth?" They were days away from home and scheduled to be on patrol for another three weeks.

"Yes, back to Earth." Uncle Wu didn't bother to disguise his impatience. "If there are any issues, refer them to me. Best possible speed back to Earth as soon as you have the package."

"May I ask what is in the package?"

"You may not!" Wu's forehead creased and his face reddened. "I'm sorry, Nephew. This is a very important issue that requires all of your attention. I can only trust this to a family member."

"You may rely on me, Uncle." Xiao hesitated. "May I ask about the size of the package? Any special handling requirements?"

Wu's face relaxed. "The cargo is small, no larger than a briefcase. As for special handling, I want you to keep it with you at all times—all times, nephew. No one is to open or tamper with the case in any way."

"I understand, Uncle. Is there anything else?"

"Yes. The ship you will be meeting, the *Renegade*, has cloaking technology. Be very wary of them; these people are not trustworthy. Also, they will expect payment on delivery."

"How do you want me to handle that?"

"I'm sending you an account with enough credits to cover the exchange. Pay them if you must, but as soon as you have the package in your possession, I want you to destroy the *Renegade*."

Xiao kept his face still. Now he knew why Uncle Wu had

called him. "You want me to use Project Moscow?"

Wu's face split in a smile, a rare occurrence for the Chinese premier. "Exactly, Nephew. I knew I could count on you."

The Project Moscow weapons were knockoffs of the Russian laser technology. Inferior to China's, of course, but perfect for blaming the demise of this unfortunate smuggler on the Russians.

Xiao bowed his head again.

"It shall be done, Uncle."

Chapter 6

White House, Washington, DC

Senator Franklin Delano Beauregard III took his time as he entered the East Room of the White House. He allowed a bemused smile to grace his carefully sculpted features.

All this for little ol' me.

"Senator, so nice of you to join us." The president's wife was a beautiful woman, and Franklin was sure the president had sent her over to soften him up.

"Milly, the opportunity to see you makes it all worthwhile." He kissed the First Lady's hand, holding onto it just a moment longer than was necessary.

She extracted her fingers but winked at him all the same. For a split second, Franklin wondered if the worm that occupied the Oval Office would stoop so low as to pimp out his own wife. No, Franklin decided, even he wouldn't go that far.

"FDB, I'm glad you came." The voice came from behind Franklin. *The worm himself, making a sneak attack from the rear.*

Franklin ran a hand over his mane of thick gray hair—the best money could buy—and energized his smile. "Mr.

President, I do believe you were about to stab me in the back, sir. You can't sneak up on an old man like that."

He swung to face the leader of the free world. Quentin Chamberlain was the definition of a compromise candidate. Hell, Franklin thought, taking in the president's weak chin and watery eyes, he even looks like a compromise candidate. Get some cosmetic surgery, man.

"Now, FDB, that's not fair," the president replied, using Franklin's nickname from the Senate, a moniker of respect that was usually reserved for members of Franklin's own party—of which the president most definitely was not. "And you're not old, either."

"Maybe you'd allow me to wet my whistle, Mr. President?" Franklin said, trying to steer the conversation to safer waters.

"Where are my manners, FDB!" He snapped his fingers at a waiter. "And please, we're after hours here; call me Quentin, just for tonight." He winked at Franklin, who did his best not to grimace back. A wink from Milly was a welcome surprise; from her husband it was just pandering.

"Why, that is very kind of you, Quentin." The waiter was back in a flash with a tumbler of bourbon. Franklin drank deeply. His eyebrows went up. Thirty-year-old small-batch Wild Turkey Kentucky Reserve—the good stuff, no longer available on the open market.

The president was watching his reaction, and he grinned. "I got it right, didn't I?" He nudged Franklin with his elbow. "That stuff is not cheap, you know."

Franklin closed his eyes, letting the bourbon roll around on his tongue. The only thing that would make this moment sweeter was if this idiot would shut up and let him enjoy his drink in peace. He opened his eyes and Quentin Chamberlain was still there. Worse yet, Milly was gone.

"Why don't we get you another one of those and let's duck into a separate room for a little chat, FDB?"

Franklin sighed. "I'd be delighted, Quentin."

***

Kyla Torres, the National Security Advisor, was waiting for them. She was a good choice for this meeting, Franklin grudgingly admitted to himself. Torres was probably the one person in the entire Chamberlain administration that he respected.

Torres rose when they entered the room. "Good evening, gentlemen." Everything about her, from her sensible haircut to her sensible shoes, radiated competence and confidence. No flash, just substance, a rarity these days.

Her hand was cool when he shook it and she met his eyes without hesitation. Then the president ruined the moment by talking.

"I think we all know why we're here, FDB."

Franklin sipped his drink and sat down. This man was totally ruining his buzz.

"If I may, Senator?" Torres's voice was low and even. She touched a button and a hologram popped out of the tabletop. The 3-D image expanded into a representation of the solar system and zoomed into the open space around Mars. A series of highlighted pods, like pickets, flashed on the display.

GILD, or Global Intelligent Laser Defense, was Franklin's baby. An interactive drone platform equipped with ultra-high-power lasers, the system was designed to operate independently in space to protect a designated area. The problem was the independent part. The CIA analysts had blown the system capabilities way out of proportion, claiming that GILD would allow artificial intelligence to fight our wars and predicting an end-of-days scenario where machines turn on their makers.

Franklin realized that both the president and Torres were waiting for him to speak. He put down his drink and settled for the truth. "I don't know what you want me to say, Quentin."

Torres shot the president a look at the use of his first name, but Chamberlain waved it off. "We're all friends here, Kyla. Let's just have a frank discussion about the pros and cons of the vote tomorrow."

"Yes, sir," Torres replied, but her lips were set in a thin line.

The president leaned his elbows on the table. "FDB, if you vote to turn this system on, I fear we're crossing a line which we won't be able to uncross."

"You mean the machines are going to take over the world, Quentin?" Franklin threw back his head and laughed. The sound bounced off the walls of the conference room. "That's a fairy tale invented by the admirals to keep up the defense budget. It's a new age, Quentin, and we've got to keep up."

"But that's just the point, Senator," Torres interrupted. "We're not keeping up, we're setting a new standard in warfare. The fact that we built the system is bad enough, but if we turn it on, then the Russians and the Chinese will be forced to deploy their own drone platforms. There's no scenario I can see where AI laser drone-ships make our solar system a safer place for anyone."

Franklin sipped the last of his bourbon and tipped the glass at the president. A flash of annoyance crossed Chamberlain's face, but he tapped a note into the tablet on the table. Franklin pretended to consider Torres's point of view before he spoke.

"So you want us to spend billions of credits on GILD, then not deploy it? Just let it rot underneath the surface of Mars? That's your plan?"

Torres shrugged. "If it were my choice, we'd never have built it in the first place, but to answer your question: yes, we let it rot. Our enemies don't even know we have it—and they never will."

Franklin started to work up a healthy dose of indignation, but his drink arrived just then and he focused on that instead. "No," he said after a long sip.

"FDB," the president said. "Please reconsider. As you vote, so goes the rest of the committee. You are potentially starting us on an arms race that our children's children will have to deal with."

Franklin shook his head. "It will leapfrog the Russians, give us the edge we need to put those Commie bastards in their place once and for all. We can lower defense spending on manned ships by half within the next decade. Half!" The bourbon came dangerously close to slopping out of the tumbler, but he saved it at the last second.

Torres and Chamberlain exchanged glances. "What will it take, FDB?" the president said. "Everything's on the table. Tell me what I can offer to convince you to vote against deploying GILD."

Franklin stared at him. Damn, but he was drunk.

"Nothing," he said.

"Pardon?" the president said.

"Nothing," Franklin repeated. The bourbon must have given him the clarity he needed. He'd come to this meeting fully prepared to bargain away his vote for the list of demands he had in his pocket, but now . . .

"There's nothing you can offer me to change my mind, Mr. President. This is a vote of conscience." *Where had that come from?* "GILD is the right thing to do for our country and our people and I fully intend to vote for it tomorrow."

Torres refused to give up. "Senator, I know you're a big supporter of the—"

Franklin held up his hand and stood. He swayed the tiniest bit. "Madam, I'm sorry, but I've made up my mind. I am voting for GILD deployment tomorrow. I bid you both a good evening." He made an abrupt about-face and marched to the door.

Chapter 7

ISS *Invincible*
Edge of Yalta Sector

"The *Leningrad* is changing course again, ma'am," said Ensign Proctor.

Addison watched the viewscreen where the ensign had plotted the Russian ship's movements. Overlaid on a map of occupied space, the RSS *Leningrad* was moving in a regular zigzag pattern.

"Looks like they're searching for something," Addison said.

"Or someone," came Captain Baltasar's voice.

"Captain on the bridge," called out the sentry at the lift doors. Addison stood, making a mental note to chew out the marine after watch. As Executive Officer, she liked to know where the captain was at all times.

"As you were, people," Baltasar said. "Talk to me, XO. What are the Russkies up to now?"

"We think it's a search pattern, sir, but we have no idea what they're after."

Baltasar pursed his lips. He pointed to the demilitarized

zone where the Yalta Sector met Chinese space. "Looks like they're headed here." Addison had a hard time seeing how he came to that conclusion. The *Leningrad* could be going anywhere.

The captain slid into his command chair and used the controls on the armrest to zero in on the DMZ. "Proctor, focus your search here."

The ensign frowned. "That's on the outer limits of sensor range, sir. Anything I get will be ghost images at best."

"Hmm—you're right, Ensign," Baltasar said. "Helm, come to new course two-four-zero, mark three. Full impulse."

Addison consulted her screen. "Captain, that takes us into Russian-controlled space."

"I'm aware, XO."

"But Captain, that's not permitted—"

"We have new tasking, XO." Baltasar's eyes were bright, and he was smiling. Not a happy smile, more like a creepy, preoccupied smile.

"I wasn't aware of any new tasking, sir."

"Well, now you know, Commander."

"Yes, sir." Addison sat back in her chair, still uneasy. It was possible that new orders had come in eyes-only for the CO, but she would have still been notified of the incoming transmission even if the content was restricted.

"Captain, you're right, sir," said Proctor in an excited voice. "There's two ships in that sector, a Chinese warship and a smaller vessel. The Russians have seen them, too. They are inbound at full power."

A light blinked on Addison's panel, indicating they had just crossed into Russian-controlled space.

The captain's fingers tightened on his armrest. "Helm, lay in a course to intercept the *Leningrad*. Full power."

The captain looked at her, his eyes bright.

"General quarters, XO."

Chapter 8

White House, Washington, DC

The cocktail party was just beginning to wind down. Franklin scanned the room for press. He wasn't actually drunk, but the last thing he needed was some bullshit blogger posting a story about his meeting with the president. If he played his cards right, he could garner a huge amount of press coverage tomorrow when the existence of GILD went public.

He found a table by the window and flagged a waiter. "The president had a bottle of Kentucky Reserve opened for me. Please bring me a glass." Franklin held his thumb and forefinger apart to show a generous measure, then he peered out the window into the swelter of a DC summer evening.

"May I join you, Senator?" The voice belonged to a young woman. Curly blonde hair, athletic build, and blue eyes the color of washed-out denim. Her dress clung to her body in all the right places.

Franklin tried to place her face and failed, so he flashed her his million-credit smile and held out his hand. "I don't believe I've had the pleasure, Miss . . ."

"Call me Angel." Her grip was firm and she held onto his

hand much longer than was necessary. Interesting . . .

"Angel? I must say, the name fits."

She laughed, a rich chuckle that intrigued Franklin even more. "I'm a longtime admirer, Senator."

The waiter showed up with a fresh drink. Franklin could tell from the color that it was not the Reserve. "What is this?" he said, aware that the woman was watching him. "I ordered the Kentucky Reserve."

The young man flushed. "I'm sorry, sir, the president has closed that bottle for the evening."

Angel laid her hand on Franklin's arm. His skin tingled with the contact. "Allow me, Senator." She slipped her arm around the waiter's waist and walked him back to the bar. As Franklin watched, she engaged the bartender in a conversation, then slipped a packet of cash into his hand. When she returned to his table, she was carrying a half-full bottle of Wild Turkey Kentucky Reserve and a single glass.

"My dear, I am impressed" was all Franklin could say.

Angel poured two fingers' worth and handed him the glass. "Like I said, Senator, I'm an admirer."

Franklin took a sip. The drink really was heavenly, and the presence of this remarkable woman made it even better. She was standing just inside his personal space, almost inviting him to bump into her.

She plucked the glass from his hand and took a sip. "I don't know anything about bourbon, Franklin. Tell me what I'm supposed to be feeling." She nudged him in the thigh with her hip.

"Bourbon is an acquired taste, Angel," Franklin said, very aware of how close she was to him. Her perfume was understated, like a hint of sweet musk, and it somehow matched the whiskey notes. Probably laced with pheromones. He'd read about that somewhere.

"I see." She took another sip and he watched her lips slide off the rim of the glass. "Perhaps you could . . . teach me, Franklin?" She handed him the glass back.

The senator surveyed the room. The party was definitely ending. If he was going to make a move, the time was now. He leaned toward Angel. "I'm an excellent teacher, Angel, but my methods take time . . ."

Angel pulled the glass out of his hand and swallowed the remainder of the bourbon. She picked up the bottle. "Then I guess school's in session, Senator." She walked away slowly, as if knowing his eyes were tracking her backside.

At the curb, Franklin signaled his limo and they ducked inside. Angel rubbed against him in the backseat, her fingers caressing the surgical implants in his pectoral muscles.

Washington, DC, at night flashed by outside the tinted window, a blur of colors that matched the rush of emotions in his head—and the rest of his body. As a confirmed bachelor and public figure, he was never without a date, but this woman was different. She poured another two fingers of Reserve into a glass and they shared it between deep kisses.

The limo drew to halt in front of his Georgetown address. Christ, he hadn't been this drunk in forever, and the presence of this beautiful creature made it seem like an exotic dream. Somehow they made it up the steps together and into the front room.

Angel took over, flipping the coffee table out of the way as if it were made of cardboard. Then she slowly drew her dress over her head and tossed it onto the couch. Wearing only a thong, she sashayed to the sideboard, found a crystal tumbler, and splashed a healthy measure of the Reserve into the glass. Franklin found himself staring at the tattoo between her shoulder blades, a dragon that shimmered in the bit of streetlight filtering in between the drapes.

"You'd better be undressed by the time I turn around," she said over her shoulder. Franklin was shaking with anticipation as he ripped off his shirt and stepped out of his trousers. In moments like this, the endless rounds of cosmetic surgery were worth every penny.

Angel turned around, her breasts swaying slightly. Franklin's mouth went dry. She was magnificent. Angel dipped her index finger in the bourbon and then slid it into her mouth, her cheeks hollowing under the suction. "I'm ready for my first lesson, Senator."

She came at him slowly, advancing until her nipples poked against his torso. His skin quivered with anticipation. She held the glass so he could take a sip. "Drink," she said but held onto the tumbler.

The bourbon was like warm sugar on his tongue, exploding his senses open.

"Lie down," she commanded.

The rug had been a gift from a Bedouin sheik many years ago. As Franklin's shoulders sank into the plush of the carpet, he wondered what the prince would think of what was about to happen on his gift.

Angel stood over him, her face in shadows. She wormed her foot between his legs, making Franklin catch his breath. Angel sipped the bourbon, then knelt down next to him. She leaned over him, allowing her breasts to graze his chest.

"Are you ready, Senator?" she whispered.

Franklin nodded, unable to trust his voice.

She gazed down at his crotch and chuckled richly. "Yes, I can see you are." She straddled him in one motion. He gasped when he felt the heat of her groin on his midsection. "But before we begin, I have a question for you."

"Anything," Franklin panted.

"How do you plan to vote tomorrow?"

Franklin fought through the fog of the alcohol. "Excuse me?"

Angel laughed again, but it had lost some of its playfulness. "Your vote," she said. "Are you voting to turn on GILD tomorrow?"

She had her hands on either side of his head, leaning over, her voice still husky with promise.

"That's confidential," he said. "How do you know about that?"

Angel shook her head. "No secrets between us, Franklin. I'm about to give you the best night of your life." She rocked her body so that her breasts bumped against his chin. "C'mon, you can tell me."

"Fine. I'm voting for GILD deployment."

Angel kissed him then, a long, deep kiss that let him know he'd made the right choice. She broke off to let him catch his breath, nibbling on his ear. "I'm sorry, Senator, but that's the wrong answer."

Franklin felt a prick on his neck. He tried to buck her off but she had wrapped her arms around his head. His heart raced, his pulse hammered uncontrollably in his ears, and his breath went shallow and fast.

As the darkness began to close in, she relaxed her grip. Angel sat up and kissed him on the forehead like he was a child.

"The Kremlin sends its regards, Senator."

Chapter 9

SS *Renegade* – Bridge
Russian–Chinese DMZ

Laz entered the bridge, determined to keep calm in front of his crew. Showtime, he thought.

"Alright, Mimi, let's see who our customer is."

Mimi made a face. "You're not gonna like it, Captain." She tapped her console and the image of an enormous Chinese warship filled the screen. "Meet the CSS *Yangtze*, the latest in destructive beauty, commanded by none other than the Chinese premier's nephew."

Laz grunted in reply. At least now they knew this whole thing had a political dimension, not that it mattered. He heard the heavy tread of Topper and Little Dick's boots on the deck plates and their sharp intake of breath when they saw the warship on the screen.

He knew how they felt. The Chinese went to great lengths to make their ships *look* deadly, with stylized curves and flashy details that had an emotional impact on the viewer.

"Nothing to see here, gentlemen," Laz said without turning around. "Meet me outside Airlock One. I'll handle the financial details." He put a hand on Mimi's shoulder. She trembled under his touch. "Let's do this. Uncloak and hail the *Yangtze*."

A man with a bald, bullet-shaped head replaced the warship on the screen. Young, Laz thought. Really young for command of a cruiser.

"*Yangtze*, this is Captain Lazarus Scollard of the SS *Renegade*."

Bullet Head nodded. "*Captain* Scollard." He made Laz's rank sound like a question. "I am Captain Sun. I believe you have something that belongs to me."

"You pay for it, you can have it," Laz shot back. Cheeky bastard.

"You will transfer the package to me, *Renegade*."

Laz sighed. "Captain Sun, I believe maybe we got off on the wrong foot. I will be very happy to arrange a transfer *after* I receive my money."

"Stand by, Scollard." The lack of respect was starting to make Laz really dislike this guy. "You should see half the agreed-on amount in your numbered account," Captain Sun said.

Mimi was already hammering away on the comms panel. She looked up, her eyes bright, mouthing, "Two point five million."

"Thank you, Sun," Laz said, returning the favor of disrespect. "We're ready to receive your shuttle."

Captain Sun's blank forehead creased into a frown. "You will bring the package to me, Scollard!"

"No can do, sir. We'll leave the airlock open for you." He signaled to Mimi to cut the transmission.

She was staring at him with something like respect. "Is it wise to bait him like that?" she said. "Two point five mill is worthless if we're dead."

Laz stared at the blank screen. "As long as we have the package we're fine. My worry is what happens after we turn it over. Your only concern right now is to get us out of here the second I tell you. No hesitation."

***

Airlock One was outfitted with a universal docking ring, but the entrance was only wide enough for personnel. The last thing Laz wanted to see was a Chinese military craft on his shuttle bay, probably filled with Chinese commandos.

As they heard the shuttle from the *Yangtze* start the docking process, he arranged Topper and Little Dick so they had an unimpeded field of fire on the airlock door. When the light on the panel turned green, Laz opened the door.

A single Chinese officer stood in the doorway. He made a stiff bow. "I am Lieutenant Commander Wei of the Chinese —"

"Yeah, I'm not interested, Commander. Let's get the rest of the money sent and this is all yours." He held up the silver case.

"Very well, Captain Scollard." Wei signaled to someone behind him in the shuttle. "The balance of your payment is in transit now."

Laz raised his voice. "Mimi, tell me the minute you see the money show up."

The seconds felt like hours. The Chinese officer stood with

his hands clasped in front of him, waiting patiently. The case seemed to weigh more by the minute. Laz felt it dragging his arm toward the floor. Finally, he couldn't take it anymore.

"Mimi," he said, his voice sounding louder than he'd intended. "Status."

She answered with a half-giggle. "The money's there, Laz. Five mill!" Topper and Little Dick hooted at each other. Laz smiled and started to hand the case over when Mimi screeched over the intercom: "Holy shit, Laz! We've got Russians inbound!"

The eyes of the Chinese officer went round with fear. "Give me the case, Captain Scollard. You have your money. Give it to me!"

Laz hesitated. There was obviously a double-cross going down somewhere in this deal and he held the trump card. Giving it away might not be the best move. Still, they'd paid the price; his job was done.

He tossed the case to the Chinese officer. "Good luck, sir. I think you're going to need it."

The man said nothing, just disappeared into the airlock hatch. Laz listened to the Chinese shuttle undock, then called out to Mimi. "He's clear, Mimi. Drop the cloak and get us the hell out of here."

The ship shuddered, knocking Laz off his feet. Someone was firing at them?

"Mimi, are we hit? Status!"

Her voice was unnaturally calm. "Yeah, we're hit. Port side nacelle, not fatal. But you need to get up here. This is getting weird."

***

When Laz was at Fleet Academy, a large portion of the advanced officer training was battle tactics. Instructors ran endless simulations of how the Chinese and Russian fleets fought, all the while pointing out their strengths and weaknesses.

But those were simulations; this was real.

The RSS *Leningrad* had as much style as a brick shithouse. Blunt-nosed and bristling with firepower, it made the *Yangtze* look delicate by comparison. The Russian swept across the bow of the Chinese ship, raking it with laser fire, leaving a furrow of melted steel across the smooth surface. The *Yangtze* was backing down, trying desperately to recover its shuttle and the precious package.

"The Russian clipped us with a single rail gun round," Mimi said. "We can cloak, but we're bleeding plasma. They'll find us in a heartbeat."

Laz punched the intercom and ordered Gizmo to get on a repair of the damaged nacelle.

The *Yangtze* had finally recovered her shuttle and the delicate ship spun on a dime, releasing a devastating barrage of bright red laser fire at the Russian ship. There was a puff of vapor and debris as the Russian's hull was breached. Russian rail gun slugs rained down on the Chinese vessel, raising a field of tiny geysers as atmosphere vented into space.

Laz had seen enough. "Bring us about and let's get the hell out of here," he said.

Mimi shook her head. "You haven't seen the best part." She pointed at the screen. "Here comes the cavalry."

A *Constitution*-class starship blazed across the screen, dwarfing both the Russian and Chinese ships. "Oh my God," he heard Little Dick say behind him. "It's huge."

"The *Invincible*," Laz said.

The *Yangtze* was in bad shape, Laz could see. She was trailing a long stream of vapor and plasma, and her lasers seemed to be offline. The *Leningrad* pressed her advantage, crisscrossing the enemy hull with laser fire. A ripple of explosions started at the rear of the *Yangtze*, then progressed forward. Escape pods popped off the hull.

The *Invincible* unleashed a continuous broadside of rail gun fire on the Russian, who was also damaged. "The *Leningrad* is sending out a mayday call," Mimi said, wonder in her voice. Still, the *Invincible* did not let up, pouring laser fire into the damaged areas. Suddenly, the Russian ship exploded in a burst of atmosphere.

"Mimi, we've overstayed our welcome," Laz said. "Drop the cloak and—"

Too late.

"Unidentified merchant ship, this is ISS *Invincible*. Stand down. Prepare to be taken on board. Acknowledge."

Mimi looked up at him. Laz felt the ship—his ship—shudder as the *Invincible*'s tractor beam locked onto them.

Laz tapped the comms console.

"*Invincible*, this is merchant ship *Renegade*. Acknowledged."

Chapter 10

Research Station
Alpha Centauri

Stacy Vallens never expected to be an astrophysicist. It just sort of happened. She retargeted the array on the dying star they were recording. Her mother had been horrified when Stacy told her about the job on Alpha Centauri. The poor woman saw the possibility of grandchildren disappearing over the horizon.

But lately, Stacy was starting to wonder if Mom had been right. A year ago, this kind of research had kept her up late at night parsing data and building models, but now . . .

She'd just turned thirty-nine, and suddenly everything seemed different. Stacy found herself looking at the social media streams of her friends from college and crying over pictures of their children. Crying! What the hell was wrong with her?

One thing she knew was that this unmet need was not going to be fulfilled on the AC, as they liked to call Alpha Centauri. Of the twelve scientists on the station, there was no one in this lot who she had even the slightest interest in.

The array beeped at her. What the hell was wrong with this stupid thing today? This was the third time she'd adjusted it this shift.

Data Interference, the readout said.

She cursed to herself and pulled up the array screen details.

"What the heck is going on?" she muttered. The meta-space band readings were fluctuating wildly. She pushed across the room on her wheeled chair to the sensors station. They used it rarely, mostly when supply ships were inbound. She powered it on, waiting for the sensors to do an initial sweep.

Stacy thought about calling Dr. Strauss but decided against it. Better to wait until she actually had something to tell him.

The sensor panel blinked, indicating the sweep was done. "Okay, boys and girls, let's see what's out there." She opened the data screen.

Stacy could scarcely believe her eyes. Five ships were closing in on the station. Five. Of unknown origin. Her hand shook as she keyed the all-station intercom.

"Everyone, this is Stacy. We have ships inbound. Um . . . I think maybe they're aliens." She closed her eyes. Someday a historian was going to write about this moment and her words "Um . . . I think maybe they're aliens" would immortalize this moment.

The room filled rapidly with the station scientists in various stages of undress and bedhead. There were protocols for this sort of thing, of course. Dr. Strauss, as the ranking scientist, took charge.

"Send out the universal greeting," he said, his voice still rusty with sleep.

The universal greeting was a package of language, math symbols, artwork, anything that might trigger a friendly response in a First Contact situation. "Broadcasting universal greeting on all channels, Doctor," said Lenny, his husband. They'd been married for twenty years, but Lenny was always scrupulous about calling his spouse "Doctor" whenever they were on duty together.

"We're getting a response, Dr. Strauss," Stacy called out.

"Put it on speaker, Dr. Vallens."

Stacy punched the button and a low droning sound filled the room. Everyone went quiet, listening.

"Run it through the translator program, Lenny," Dr. Strauss said.

Minutes ticked by. The sound grew louder, more intense.

"Nothing," Lenny said.

"I have a visual, Doctor," Stacy said. Strauss nodded at her.

The alien ships were arranged in a diamond formation. The one in front had large openings on either side, like air scoops on a jet.

"Hot damn," someone said. Another person laughed and said, "They're beautiful." Stacy felt a thrill race up her spine. They were famous. After twenty-four centuries of wondering if mankind was alone in the universe, the people in this room were the first to make contact with an alien life form. Around her, Stacy saw a few of the scientists finger-comb their hair, suddenly aware their images would be part of history forever.

"Standby to transmit the First Contact report," Dr. Strauss said. The report was a preformatted message to notify UEF CENTCOM that someone, after centuries of space travel, had finally found life in the universe. "Append a recording of this transmission. Anyone have anything to add?"

"Sounds like bees," Stacy volunteered, then immediately regretted saying it. To her surprise, Dr. Strauss looked her way, nodding.

"You're right, Stacy, that's exactly what it sounds like. Like a swarm of bees. Put that in the message."

"Standing by to transmit, Dr. Strauss," called the scientist manning the comms panel.

"Transmit," said Dr. Strauss.

"Nothing happened," the man on comms said. "I think we're being jammed."

"Try again," said Strauss, his voice hitching up a notch with tension.

"Still nothing."

"Load the message onto a probe and send it," Strauss said. "Do it now."

Seconds ticked by as the ships on the screen got larger and the buzzing sound intensified.

"Probe away, Doctor."

"Good." Strauss had moved so he was behind Lenny and he placed his hands on his husband's shoulders. They were both staring at the screen; they all were. Lenny's hand crept up to link fingers with his lover.

Stacy thought about babies. Little pink babies with soft skin and happy giggles. To her surprise, she found that her cheeks were wet. Strauss caught her eye and smiled at her.

"Look," someone said.

The lead vessel filled most of the viewscreen now and they could see clearly the openings on either side of the ship. The open space seemed to shimmer, then hundreds of tiny flying figures poured into space.

The droning noise became a physical vibration that Stacy could feel in the soles of her feet. The air in the room felt thick, and she could hear someone praying out loud. The first shots from the alien fighters rumbled in the distance, more felt than heard.

Stacy Vallens closed her eyes and pictured the babies she would never have.

Chapter 11

ISS *Invincible* – Flight Deck

Addison Halsey planted herself in front of her commanding officer. "Captain, we need to discuss what just happened out there. You just blew up a Russian warship."

Captain Baltasar looked past her toward the hangar. "Not now, XO."

"Captain, that was an act of war. We just violated a couple centuries of peace treaties without even so much as a conversation with CENTCOM."

Baltasar pinned her with his trademark icy glare, but Addison had no intention of backing down. Not this time. "XO, let me tell you what I saw. The Russians were firing on a Chinese warship. I was lending aid to an ally. The loss of the *Leningrad* was collateral damage to our actions."

Addison gaped at him. The breadth of the lie was beyond comprehension. The *Invincible* had come in guns blazing. "Sir, we do not have permission to use offensive weapons in—"

"XO, this conversation is over. I will file my report with CENTCOM as soon as we see what all the fuss was about with this merchant ship." He turned his attention to the crewman operating the tractor beam. "Drop it in the center of the hangar. Have the marines standing by in case we need to do a forced entry."

Addison looked over the ship specs on the screen. SS *Renegade*, Caliphate-registered. Merchant, my ass, she thought. These guys were nothing but outlaws, modern-day space pirates. What the hell were they doing in the DMZ caught in the crossfire between the Russians and the Chinese?

"How many crew?" she asked the operator.

"Five, ma'am. They're armed, too."

The captain pressed the transmit button. "*Renegade*, this is Captain Baltasar of the ISS *Invincible*. You have thirty seconds to surrender or I'm sending in my marines."

"No need to get violent, Captain," said a male voice. "We're coming out with our hands up."

Addison started. That voice . . . it couldn't be. *No way*.

"Problem, XO?" The captain was looking at her through narrowed eyes.

"No, sir. Just thinking about the Russians, sir."

Baltasar grunted. "Let's go meet our guests."

The ramp of the *Renegade* was just touching the hangar deck by the time they reached the ship. Five figures made their way slowly down the incline, hands half raised. The captain waved off the marines.

Addison swept her eyes over the group of prisoners. A muscle-bound black man with blond hair, a bald giant with a vacant stare, a slight bespectacled older guy in dirty overalls, and a slim, raven-haired woman. And *him*.

Lazarus Scollard. She hadn't seen him for the better part of two decades, but time had been kind to him. He still had the same square jaw and ever-present half-smile as if he were hearing a dirty joke in the background.

He stopped cold when he saw her. The smile slipped away. "Addie," he said.

Baltasar's head snapped toward her. "Addie? You two know each other?"

Addison flushed. No one called her Addie. Not since him, at least.

"Captain Baltasar, allow me to introduce Lazarus Scollard. Fleet Academy washout. Honor violation."

"Laz." Scollard stepped forward with his hand outstretched. Baltasar stared until he dropped his hand.

"Honor violation, huh?" Baltasar said. "And now you're a pirate. Congratulations, you've managed to lower your standards."

To Addison's surprise, Laz shrugged. "I've made my peace with my mistakes." He looked at her. "Maybe the rest of you should, too."

Addison felt herself redden.

"Why were you in the DMZ, Scollard?" Baltasar asked.

Laz shrugged again. "Pirate business."

Baltasar's fist lashed out, connecting with Laz's jaw. The man sank to one knee.

Addison stepped forward. "Captain, we—"

"I'll ask again, Scollard," Baltasar said. "Why were you in the DMZ?"

Laz got to his feet, rubbing his jaw.

"Like I said, we had business there."

"What kind of business?"

The crew of the *Renegade* stirred, but Laz waved them back.

"We were delivering a package, if you must know. Nothing illegal, just a simple courier service."

"What was in the package?"

When Laz smiled, his teeth were bloody. "Guess we'll never know, Captain. We gave the package to the Chinese, who got blown up by the Russians, who got blown up by you. Whatever was in the package is long gone."

"You're lying," Baltasar said.

"Nope," Laz smiled at the captain again as if baiting the man to punch him again.

But he was lying. Laz might be able to pull off deceit like a pro, but the rest of his crew were amateurs. Addison saw the woman exchange an uneasy glance with the black guy. Baltasar saw it, too.

"You." He pointed at the woman. "What's your name, miss?"

"Mimi. Mimi Ferreira."

Baltasar beckoned her closer. "Okay, Mimi, your captain is headed to the brig for trafficking in stolen property. You want to join him?"

"Mimi . . ." Laz said.

The woman set her chin. "It was some kind of biological material. A case with twelve test tubes. That's all I know."

"And you gave it to the Chinese?"

"Yeah . . . except Laz kept one sample."

"Dammit, Mimi," Laz muttered.

"Thank you, Miss Ferreira." Baltasar signaled to the marine standing by. "Take the ship apart, gentlemen, until you find that sample."

"That won't be necessary, Captain," Laz said. He reached

into his breast pocket and pulled out a glass vial.

Baltasar took the tube and held it carefully in his cupped hands. "That's the first smart thing you've done so far, Scollard. Let's hope it's not the last." He nodded to the marines. "Put them in the brig, Sergeant." The captain seemed preoccupied with the vial in his hand.

"Hey!" Mimi said when one of the marines tried to grab her arm. "What about me?"

Baltasar made a motion like he was swatting a fly, his attention still on the tube.

"Put her in the brig, too."

Chapter 12

ISS *Eagle* – Captain's Ready Room
Orbiting Ganymede Station

Captain Luke Mannix surveyed the rest of the "Welcoming Committee," as they'd dubbed themselves. The meeting was for commanding officers only, but the COs were permitted to have their senior staff listen in if they wanted. Most of them did, he was sure.

"You've read the incredibly thin intelligence report from the research crew on the AC. Not much to go on." He paused, watching their faces. They were a good group—on paper. But like every other person in the room, he knew that the UEF hadn't fired a shot in anger since the First Interstellar War in the twenty-third century. How would these men and women react under real battle stress? Hell, how would *he* react in a real battle situation?

Mannix cracked a smile. "This is not how I expected First Contact to feel." Nervous smiles went around the room like a virus. From the very first year in Fleet Academy, they were drilled on First Contact protocol, a doctrine written by a bunch of well-meaning eggheads who most definitely did not want mankind's first alien encounter to go down in history as a bloodbath.

Mannix stood, pacing at the head of the room. "We don't know what happened at the AC. Maybe they're all fine and their comms gear has been disabled somehow. I'd like to believe that, but in our profession hope is not a strategy, it's a fast way to a pine box. In my opinion, the research station at Alpha Centauri was overrun by these—what are we calling them again?"

"The Swarm," said Gretchen Kang, captain of the *Defiant*. She was commanding a light destroyer, but Mannix was confident that with Gretchen in command the *Defiant* would punch well above its weight class. She was a short woman with the stature of a wrestler but always with a ready smile.

"The Swarm," Mannix mused. The droning noise they projected was unnerving. The analysts even speculated it could be a weapon of some kind. He blew out a long breath. It was time to level with this crew.

"Ladies and gentlemen, it's time to talk turkey, as we used to say back in the day. We are the welcoming committee for the incoming Swarm ships. Our optimistic scenario is that we will be able to communicate with these beings." What would an alien look like? he wondered. His mind had been so polluted by thousands of sci-fi vids that he feared he'd miss some vital clue and start an intergalactic massacre.

"That's the optimistic scenario." He paused for effect. "But I'm a pessimist by nature. The downside possibility is that we're looking at an invasion force. If that's the case, then we have a job to do. A big job."

Six ships, that's all they'd been able to muster to Ganymede

Station on short notice. It had not gone unnoticed that the Swarm had managed—either by sheer dumb luck or by design —to stay inside the limits of UEF space. Another question that the intel teams back at CENTCOM had not been able to answer.

"We are the welcoming committee for new neighbors. The Russians and the Chinese have opted to let us handle First Contact." He offered the crowd a bleak smile. "That might give you some insight into how they think this is going to go down."

"Bastards," Gretchen muttered.

Mannix nodded. "Here's our battle plan," he said. When he touched his tablet, a 3-D hologram jumped out of the center of the table. Ganymede looked like a golf ball next to the massive bulk of Jupiter. "We will sortie from G-town in one hour to meet our guests. *Eagle* will be running point. The Midwest squadron will follow in standard diamond formation on the *Defiant.*"

The Midwest squadron consisted of the *Minnesota*, *Iowa*, *Illinois*, and *Kansas*: all lightly armored frigates built for chasing pirates and running border patrols, completely unsuitable for meeting a potential alien strike force. He cursed the Russians again. Those bastards had at least two heavy cruisers within a day's travel of Ganymede. He'd give anything for a *Constitution*-class starship right now. That would make these Swarm bastards sit up and take notice.

"The *Eagle* will meet the incoming force and attempt to make contact. If we're successful, we can all crack a beer and sing campfire songs with our new friends. If—and I stress this again—*if* we engage militarily, your signal to attack will be when I launch my fighters."

Mannix cracked his knuckles one at a time, letting the popping sound echo in the silent room. "I don't want to leave you with any false feelings of hope. If this situation goes sideways, our job is to stop the Swarm. At any cost. If we can't stop them, then we need to slow them down long enough for UEF to get ready for a full-scale attack." He drew in a deep breath.

"Questions?"

There were none.

***

ISS *Eagle* **– Bridge**
UEF space near Ganymede Station

"Sir, I've got a visual on the five alien ships."

Mannix sat up in his command chair. "Very well, Sensors. On screen, high mag."

Even at full magnification, they were still pretty small in the vast emptiness of space, but he could make out five distinct vessels in an arrowhead formation.

"Let's hear what they sound like, Ensign," he said to the sensors officer.

A droning sound filled the room. The analysts had been over and over the data package from Alpha Centauri and they were split on whether this was a language or a jamming signal. Whatever it was, it sounded damn annoying to Mannix. "All right, I get the idea. You can turn it off now." The sound ceased. "Continue sending the live stream back to Earth to see if the eggheads can make heads or tails out of it."

They'd been blasting their First Contact greeting for the past hour with no reply. His minimal optimism in a nonviolent outcome had ebbed even further. It was time to get this party started.

"Open a channel to the *Defiant*."

Captain Gretchen Kang's square face appeared on the screen.

"Captain Kang, I'm about to go meet our guests," he said. "You're in command of the remaining force until I return. First strike rules of engagement apply. Understood?"

"Understood, Captain." She hesitated. "Good luck, sir."

"I don't need luck, Captain Kang," he said. "I have a fighter squadron. *Eagle*, out."

He heard the nervous titter of laughter circulate through the bridge crew. Good; they needed something to break the tension. Mannix punched the intercom.

"Bridge to Commander Johns."

"CAG here, sir." Tad "Whippet" Johns was his Commander Air Group, or CAG, in Fleet parlance.

"How're your men, Tad?"

"Young, dumb, and full of cum," Whippet replied. Another round of chuckles ran through the bridge crew. "Sorry, sir. We're in a ready flight status."

Mannix fought the grin that wanted to break out. "Thank you, Commander. Let's hope we don't need you. Bridge, out." He killed the connection.

Mannix's tongue was suddenly dry as toast. Everything he said, every movement he made in the next few moments, would be recorded and dissected by historians forever. Good or bad, he was making history.

"Helm, intercept course to the Swarm vessels. Flank speed."

The Swarm ships were huge, easily ten times the size of the *Eagle*, with huge openings on either side of the bow.

"Sensors, what's your take on construction?"

"I'm not seeing point-defense systems, sir, but what worries me is those open areas. Could be fighter bays, or some other kind of weapon."

The drone sound was audible now. Mannix could even feel a slight vibration in the hull, and it unnerved him.

"Open a channel, all frequencies." He cleared his throat. "Alien vessel, this is Captain Lucas Mannix of the ISS *Eagle*. Please respond."

The drone continued uninterrupted.

"Any change at all in that sound?" he asked the sensors station.

"No, sir." The ensign's face was pale beneath her dark bob of hair.

Mannix drew in a deep breath. His stomach was a churning cauldron of acid. "One more time, Comms."

"Channel open, sir."

"Alien vessel, this is Captain Lucas Mannix of the ISS *Eagle*. We mean you no harm. We are a peaceful people, and we welcome those who come in peace. Please respond."

The *Eagle* was no more than a hundred thousand kilometers away now, and they'd had to reduce the screen magnification to keep the alien vessels in full view.

"Sir, I'm getting a response!" the sensors station called out.

Mannix thought maybe he could sense it as well, a slightly

higher pitch to the incessant drone and a deeper thrumming bass to the signal.

"Oh my God," whispered the XO.

Mannix looked up at the screen. Hundreds of smaller vessels—fighters, he was sure of it—were pouring out of the openings of the lead ship. His stomach went still and he found his voice. He touched the intercom button on his armrest.

"CAG, this the captain. Launch fighters. You are weapons free, Commander."

Chapter 13

ISS Eagle – Red Squad Fighters

Lieutenant "Ramrod" Sturgiss shot out the *Eagle*'s fighter bay at full throttle. "Easy and Choo-choo, stay tight on me. Let's go bag some bad guys, Red Squad."

"Roger that, Ramrod." Choo-choo's normally girlish voice was low and tight with tension.

"You got it, boss." Easy's bass voice was reassuring in the mayhem.

The alien ships were everywhere, flying in no apparent formations, just . . . *swarming* was the only word he could think of. He ripped off a blast of cannon fire and nailed two of them. His wingmen were doing the same. Like shooting fish in a barrel, as his grandfather would say.

"Holy Mother of Fudge, there's a ton of them," Choo-choo said. "They're like ants." Another blast of cannon fire from his right and another alien exploded right in front of him. The debris smacked against his cockpit, leaving a spiderweb of cracks.

"Red Squad," Whippet's voice boomed in Ramrod's headset. "Get through the fighters and get us a close-up recon on the mother ship. We need to know what we're dealing with here."

"Roger that, CAG." Ramrod punched the throttle and laid on the cannon again. At this rate, he'd be out of ammo before they even made it to the mother ship.

The alien fighters were getting more numerous the closer they got to the host ship. Ramrod blasted two more aliens in his path before disaster struck. His panel flashed a warning. Projectiles streaked past his cockpit window.

"I've got one on my six," he yelled.

Easy fell away from his left side. "Break right on my mark, Ramrod. Now!" Ramrod jammed his stick over and rolled. The space behind him lit up with an explosion.

But there were two more, one on either side of him. The alien fighters closed in, crushing him between them. Ramrod used his cannon to clip the nose off the fighter on his left, but the damage to his craft was done. He jacked around in his seat, looking for Choo-choo, but she was dealing with her own devils. She blasted another fighter. "Hang on, Ramrod," she called. "I'm coming!"

An alien fighter appeared behind her. "Choo-choo, on your six!"

It was too late. His friend's craft imploded in a fiery bubble. He heard Easy cursing in a solid stream over the open net.

"Easy! On me!" Ramrod shouted. He was having trouble maintaining a steady course. One of his stabilizers must have been busted by the kamikaze run he'd just endured.

Easy appeared on his port side, flashing him a tight smile. "Let's get some pictures, boss," he said.

They burst through the last wave of alien fighters, giving them an unobstructed view of the Swarm ship. "Whippet, are you getting this?" Ramrod said.

"Yeah, Ramrod, it's coming through five-by-five." He could sense the despair in the CAG's voice. "Good job, Red Squad."

Ramrod didn't answer. Flying next to the Swarm ship was like being a mosquito on the ass of a bull elephant. The alien ship seemed to have no point defenses other than fighters. They cruised past a massive laser emplacement. He wasn't an expert on energy weapons, but it was the biggest laser he'd ever seen on any ship in his life.

"Looks like an armadillo," Easy said. Ramrod nodded. The armor on the alien ship overlapped like the scales of a living creature, each layer reinforcing the one behind it.

Ramrod was having increasing trouble with his course control. "We need to cut this short, Easy. I was hit back there and the damage is getting worse."

When they swept past the scoop opening on the side of the Swarm ship, Ramrod got a good look straight down the gullet of the alien flight deck. He gulped. Hundreds of shadowy fighters clung to the walls of the curved hangar, like bats hanging from the walls of a cave.

"There's so many," Easy whispered.

As Ramrod watched, a group of six fighters detached from the wall and swept into an organized flight pattern, heading straight for them.

Whippet's voice boomed in his ears. "Red Squad, pull out. Now!"

***

ISS *Defiant* **– Bridge**

Captain Gretchen Kang had made her peace with what was about to happen. She fingered the prayer beads on her wrist, a tiny bit of calm in the midst of the chaos around her.

"The *Eagle* is launching fighters, ma'am."

"Very well." She touched her armrest and raised her voice. "Midwest Squadron, it appears that our negotiations have not gone well. Diamond formation on me, shields at maximum." She broke the connection.

"Helm, give me an intercept course to the *Eagle*. Flank speed."

Within minutes they reached the cloud of fighters around Mannix's ship. He'd taken some damage on his port side but still looked capable. On the other hand, the *Eagle*'s fighter squadron was getting decimated.

Using shields and point-defense systems, she mowed a path through the fighters. Not pretty, but effective against the smaller craft.

"Status report," she called.

"Shields at seventy percent, ma'am. The Midwest squadron is still in formation."

"Very well. Open a channel to *Eagle*." She paused. "Captain Mannix, I'm coming up on your port side, sir. I'll engage the lead alien ship with rail guns."

"Roger that, Captain Kang. We're trying to recover fighters, but it's a losing battle. I'll join the party as soon as I can. *Eagle*, out."

Kang switched channels. "Midwest Squadron, gamma

formation. Concentrate rail gun fire on the lead ship." Acknowledgments flowed in and Gretchen saw the ships form a battle line to maximize their projectile firepower. They broke through the thickest concentration of fighters and the alien ships were clearly visible. She smiled grimly. Time for some payback for all those fighters.

"Fire on my mark," she said. "Three, two—"

A brilliant green laser shot out of the lead ship. She heard the sensors officer pull in a sharp breath. "Ma'am, I—I—the *Minnesota* and the *Iowa*, they're gone." Another bolt of green lanced out of the lead alien ship. "The *Kansas*, too."

"All rail guns, continuous fire," Kang replied. Between the incessant vibration of the Swarm and the pulsing of the rail guns, it felt like she was riding a horse. "Damage assessment."

"Surface damage only, ma'am—as far as we can tell." The laser spurted out again. "*Illinois* is gone."

The *Eagle* crossed the viewscreen, her rail guns blazing, a cloud of enemy fighters in close pursuit. A small explosion erupted on the surface of the alien ship. Kang pointed to the screen. "Weapons, target all rail gun fire on that spot."

"Aye-aye, ma'am." Gretchen noted with satisfaction that the explosion was growing into a golden ripple of fire across the hull of the alien ship.

A text message popped up on her private screen. "From Mannix: Omega Protocol in effect." She tapped out an acknowledgment.

"Ma'am, one of the other ships is moving." The sensors officer pointed to the screen. The alien ship on the port side was pulling forward to block their fire on the lead Swarm vessel.

Gretchen nodded. "I'm taking that as an acknowledgment that we're having an effect. XO, maneuver us so we can keep up the fire on the lead ship."

"Aye-aye, ma'am." The ship banked hard as the XO took control. *Eagle* had the same idea, turning in a wide arc to keep a clear line of fire on the damaged alien craft. Gretchen could see the *Eagle* had a long gash across her side—probably from laser fire—and she was leaving a trail of debris in her wake. The alien fighters had backed off, though, and her rail guns continued to pound at the lead alien ship. The blossom of damage on the hull of the massive vessel continued to expand.

The second Swarm ship began continuous laser fire on the *Eagle*, making the viewscreen glow with green light. Mannix's shields were all but gone, and the alien laser carved a broad arc across the heavy cruiser's side. More atmosphere and debris vented.

The *Eagle* accelerated toward the alien ship, toward the spot where they'd managed to cause damage.

Omega Protocol, thought Gretchen. Suicide run. She clutched at the beads on her wrist, saying a silent prayer for Mannix and his brave crew.

But it was not to be. The two alien ships concentrated all their laser fire on the *Eagle*'s engine room. Where the core was housed.

The *Eagle* evaporated in a flash of light.

The laser fire turned on the *Defiant*. The ship bucked as its shields tried to absorb the energy of the alien barrage.

"Shields at fifty percent, ma'am." The weapons officer had a note of panic in his voice. "And falling fast."

Mannix had waited too long. She would not make the same

mistake.

"Weapons, continue to target the damaged area on the lead alien ship. Shift all shields to protect the reactor core." Gretchen paused. "Helm, plot a collision course to the lead alien ship. I want us right in the middle of that damaged area."

The bridge crew were all looking at her now. She fixed the expression on her face. "I have been ordered to use the Omega Protocol." The hum of the Swarm was so loud she had to shout. "It has been an honor to serve with you all."

The sensors officer was crying quietly at her station and somewhere behind her, comms, maybe, she heard the sound of praying.

"Course laid in, ma'am," the XO shouted in her ear.

The alien laser fire slashed across the hull, and she felt a ripple under her feet as one of the decks below them vented to space.

Gretchen fingered her beads for the last time.

"Engineering, give me everything you've got. Helm, engage."

The ship leapt underneath her, but whether it was from the engines or the enemy fire, she couldn't tell.

Chapter 14

UEF Headquarters
New York City

They'd dispensed with diplomatic protocols for the meeting. Each head of state flew to New York overnight with a minimal security detail and no press entourage. None of them had slept much, if at all.

President Quentin Chamberlain surveyed the room and was not filled with hope. It said something when it felt like the most accessible person in the room was Russian President Oleksiy Ivanov, his most ardent rival.

But that was yesterday, Chamberlain told himself, before they faced mutual annihilation. Ivanov was watching him, his heavy lids and impassive features concealing a genius-level mind. Chamberlain had been briefed that the Russian was a chess grand master.

Chinese Premier Sun Wu was much more youthful than he appeared in press pictures. Given the Chinese penchant for all things ancient, they probably doctored his photos to make him look older. Sun sat with pursed lips, giving nothing away while he waited for the meeting to start.

And then there was the Supreme Leader of the Caliphate, Masoud el-Hashem. Chamberlain had half expected the famously inward-looking Caliphate to reject his request for a face-to-face meeting. But here they were. El-Hashem was dressed in simple robes of soft beige and seemed the most at ease in the room. He smiled at Chamberlain and nodded pleasantly as if they were at a cocktail party.

He'd deliberately excluded all their defense ministers and the heads of state for all the member nations of the UEF. Sure, they'd feel rejected, but unless he could get these three men on his side, it didn't matter a whit if France joined in the fight or not. They needed firepower and lots of it.

"Gentlemen," Chamberlain said. All eyes were on him. Between them, these men represented the majority of the billions of people spread across inhabited space. "Twelve hours ago, a small force of UEF Fleet ships engaged the aliens —we are calling them the Swarm. The end result was complete destruction of our forces."

Chamberlain had to force himself not to throw an accusing glare at Ivanov. That selfish Russian prick might have been able to make a difference and he'd sat on his hands.

"And what did you learn from the engagement, Quentin?" Ivanov's voice was like gravel crunching underfoot, probably from the two packs of cigarettes he smoked every day. Chamberlain resisted the urge to smack the smile off Ivanov's fat face. He took a deep breath to calm himself.

"The alien ships are equipped with large numbers of fighters and ultra-high-power lasers. They have minimal shields and are susceptible to projectile weapons. The fighters appear to be below par with ours in terms of maneuverability and firepower, but they outnumber us by an order of magnitude."

He let that sink in. Even Ivanov seemed to sober up at that assessment.

"Do we have any idea what they seek?" el-Hashem said. He had a soft voice with a musical quality to it.

Chamberlain shook his head. "All attempts at communications have gone unanswered. Based on their actions here and at Alpha Centauri, I think we can safely assume they mean us harm."

"Are you sure of that, President Chamberlain?" It was the Chinese premier. He had a commanding baritone, the kind of voice used to giving orders. "Perhaps if you had not met them with heavily armed warships you would have had a different outcome."

"If I may point out, Premier Sun, we have also lost all contact with an undefended research station on Alpha Centauri. We presume that station was wiped out."

"You presume, Mr. President," the premier persisted, "but do you know? Perhaps their communications capability has been damaged."

"Perhaps," Chamberlain admitted, "but unlikely."

Wu shrugged and Chamberlain continued.

"The purpose of this meeting is to form an alliance against what we believe is a threat to humanity—all humanity, regardless of race, creed, or political persuasion. I recommend we pool our defensive resources and meet the alien force with our combined might."

Chamberlain let his words hang in the air. They were pretty good, he had to admit. Something for the history books that he could be proud of having said.

El-Hashem spoke first. "I'm afraid the Caliphate has very little in the way of warships, Mr. President. As a theocracy, our military is mostly limited to troops and the means to move them through space."

Chamberlain nodded. That was mostly true, although the intelligence they had on the Caliphate was remarkably spotty, a result of having spent too many generations focused on the Russians and the Chinese.

"We see merit in your proposal, Mr. President," Premier Wu said. "We will participate, as long as we have an equal say in the decision-making process."

Chamberlain resisted the urge to smile. That had been much easier than he'd anticipated. His aides told him the premier would be the holdout. He turned to the Russian. "Well, Oleksiy?"

The Russian's eyes shifted beneath their heavy lids as if he was searching for an exit. Finally, he nodded. "I agree, but we need to decide something else first."

Chamberlain frowned. "I assume you mean the command structure. We've been giving that some thought and—"

"No, I mean your GILD system."

Chamberlain froze. How on earth did the Russians know about that?

"I'm not sure what you mean, Oleksiy. That's no more than some journalist's wet dream."

"Do not insult my intelligence, Mr. President. I happen to know that you were planning a vote to turn the system on this very week but some unfortunate events prevented that from happening."

Chamberlain reached for a pitcher of water, pouring

himself a glass. The liquid did nothing to quench the dryness in his mouth.

"What is this GILD system?" the Chinese premier asked.

"Space drones," Ivanov replied, clearly enjoying himself. "A high-power laser platform able to fight by itself using artificial intelligence."

Wu looked at Chamberlain. "This is true?"

The president shifted in his seat. "Oleksiy is overstating the capability, but he has the basic facts correct."

"And this system is operational now?" Wu said. The smugness was gone from his expression, replaced by a wariness.

"Potentially," Chamberlain admitted.

"It is imperative that we use the GILD system to engage the aliens before they get closer to Earth, Quentin," said the Russian.

"I disagree," said Wu. "This is the kind of weapon that will put us all in danger. I cannot support that decision."

"Premier Wu," began Chamberlain, "I believe it is in our best interest to use all of our assets in this fight."

Chinese Premier Wu stood. "Then the People's Republic of China will not be part of this alliance." He stalked out of the room.

Chapter 15

ISS *Invincible* – Briefing Room

Addison did her best not to flinch as Admiral Kilgore's voice narrated the blow-by-blow destruction of the *Eagle*, the *Defiant*, and the four ships of the Midwest Squadron. When the *Defiant* crashed into the alien vessel in a blazing explosion, The senior officer's face filled the screen.

"That's what we're dealing with, Captain Baltasar. For all the efforts of Captains Mannix and Kang and their crews, the Swarm fleet sustained minimal damage and has maintained steady course and speed toward Earth. We're recalling the entire Fleet to face this threat. We want the *Invincible* to attack the alien rear guard at Mars Station."

Captain Baltasar frowned. "Admiral, even at max g's and full inertial dampeners, we won't reach Mars by the time the Swarm gets there."

Kilgore nodded her gray head. "I know, Captain—that's why you're being authorized to perform an intra-system q-jump."

Quantum drive, technology that connected a quantum field coupler to the ship's hull, allowed a starship like the *Invincible* to "jump" through space-time. Although it had been in existence for the last fifty years as a military technology, its use was strictly regulated to open space for travel between systems.

Kilgore let that sink in. "As of this moment, we are in a state of unrestricted warfare against the Swarm. The Commander in Chief is meeting with the heads of state from Russia, China, and the Caliphate as we speak to combine our military might against these invaders."

"And we still have no idea what they want, Admiral?" Addison asked. Surely an alien race capable of interstellar travel would have managed to expend some effort on the ability to communicate.

"None," the Admiral replied. "Based on their response at Ganymede, we assume the worst."

"We understand, Admiral," Baltasar said, rising. "We will meet the Swarm at Mars."

"Before you go, Captain." Kilgore was smiling now. "We have a surprise waiting for the aliens when they reach Mars space. It should make your job much easier."

"Surprise?" Baltasar sat back down. To Addison, his face did not look like a man about to receive good news.

The screen changed again to a 3-D rendering of space around Mars with Kilgore's voice narrating again. "What I'm about to tell you is highly classified. For the past three years, there has been a top-secret program in development on Mars called GILD, or Global Intelligent Laser Defense. The unmanned system deploys an ultra-high-power laser on multiple platforms."

As she spoke, a cylinder in the screen burst apart into a series of wedge-shaped craft.

"How is it controlled?" Baltasar asked. Addison did a double-take. Her captain was pale.

"Artificial intelligence," the admiral replied. "It works off a hive mind principle, allowing each member of the collective to operate independently or in a pack. An intelligent swarm, if you will."

Addison found herself nodding along with the rest of the room. This was the first bit of good news they'd had about the alien invasion so far.

"Why wasn't I told about this before, Admiral?" Baltasar demanded.

Kilgore sat back in her chair at the captain's tone. "The very existence of this system had the potential to throw the fragile balance of power between the Earth nations into chaos. It would most likely trigger an arms race in unmanned AI warfare."

"How do we know that GILD won't turn on us during a battle?" Baltasar pressed the admiral. "If there's no human intervention, aren't we at risk for collateral damage?"

Kilgore smiled. "Relax, Captain. We have that covered. Mars will send you a safe code. As long as you transmit this code during initial contact with the GILD system, you and any fighters will be registered with GILD and remain unharmed."

Baltasar continued to shift in his seat. "Will that be all, Admiral?" he asked.

"Nearly. If you could clear the room, Captain, I need to have a word with you and your XO."

The captain stiffened in his chair, then turned slowly to Addison. "Clear the room, people," he said without taking his eyes off her.

When the room was finally empty, Admiral Kilgore cleared her throat. "Captain Baltasar, I received a very distressing after-action report from Commander Halsey. Is it true you fired on and destroyed a Russian warship?"

Baltasar's frame quivered with tension. "Admiral, I'm not sure what Addison sent you, but I can assure you we were saving an innocent merchant from certain destruction—"

"The logs that Commander Halsey sent along as supporting evidence tell a different story, Captain," the admiral interrupted.

Baltasar glowered at the screen. "Admiral, I—"

Kilgore cut him off with a chop of her hand. "Enough, Captain. The service records of both of you are exemplary and a matter of this magnitude is not something we can deal with right now. I wanted you to know that I have retained these files in my personal logs until such time as I can perform a proper investigation. As for now, I need both of you to work as a team against our common enemy: the Swarm."

Baltasar bowed his head. "I understand, Admiral."

"Commander Halsey?" The admiral directed her attention to Addison.

Addison nodded. "Yes, ma'am."

"Godspeed, *Invincible*. Kilgore out." The screen went blank.

Baltasar wheeled on her. "Do you have any idea what you've done, Commander?" His face was flushed and he pressed far into her personal space. Addison held her ground.

"What was that malarkey about saving an innocent merchant?" she shot back. "It was a smuggler and you commandeered their ship. You fired on and destroyed a Russian warship! In any other circumstances, that would have been an act of war."

Baltasar's eyes glittered, and Addison wondered if her captain had lost his marbles. Her eye caught a glint of color in his breast pocket, a glowing green.

His hand slapped at the pocket to cut off her view, but not before she saw the vial of material Baltasar had taken from Laz.

"We're finished here, Commander," he said. "I'll deal with you later. For now, make preps for the q-jump." He stalked out.

Addison let the silence of the room soak into her senses, welcoming the calm after the last few minutes of storm. She needed to find out more about this mysterious vial. She gritted her teeth.

For that, she needed to see Laz.

Chapter 16

ISS *Invincible* – Brig

The thought of seeing Laz again triggered a rush of conflicting emotions and indecision. Should she act like they had no past and he was just a prisoner? No, she needed him to open up. Should she greet him like the friend—and lover—he once was? She bristled at the thought. He'd hurt her more than anyone else in her life. There was no way she was going to forgive *that*, not in this lifetime, anyway.

In the end, it didn't matter. Laz's cell was tiny, just large enough for a fold-down bunk and a chair bolted to the floor. He was lying on the bed, eyes fixed on the ceiling. When the marine guard let her in, he sat up and said, "Addie."

It wasn't so much the word as the way he said it. He still cared, she could tell. Even after all this time and distance, he still cared.

Addison glared at him. "This is not a social call. I'm still mad at you."

He held up his hands. "Fair enough."

"And no one calls me Addie."

"I used to."

She intensified her glare, trying to put all the hateful things she'd wanted to say to him into that stare. Laz didn't flinch.

"That was a long time ago," she said finally. Was that her voice breaking? Dammit!

"Agreed." Laz looked away. "I suppose you're going to tell me why you came all the way down here to talk to a guilty man."

"What?" Addison said. "Oh, right. This cargo you were carrying. Tell me about it."

Laz pinched a tuft of his close-cropped beard and pursed his lips. "I suppose it doesn't make much difference now, so why not? It was a double-blind job." Addison gave him a blank look. "That means I didn't know who the seller or the buyer was. Strictly courier stuff. They gave me a pick-up point and a drop-off point, that's it. I was as surprised as the next guy when the Chinese showed up and even more surprised when the Russians joined the party." He smiled at her, a smile she remembered well. "And totally stunned when the *Invincible* flew in guns blazing. I suppose the Old Man is going to get relieved over that stunt, right?"

Addison realized Laz had no idea about the Swarm. When she filled him in, he sank back against the wall in stunned surprise.

"Aliens?" he said. "I never thought I'd see that day." He peered at her closely. "So why are you down here talking to me? You have a world to save, woman."

That was a good question. What *was* she doing here? When she thought logically about a connection between Captain Baltasar and Laz's cargo, it made no sense.

"I don't know exactly, Laz," she said. "But up until a day

ago, I was serving under one of the most professional commanding officers in the entire Fleet. Total hard-ass, but the best in the business. The man practically had the regs committed to memory, and then he crosses Russian-controlled space to destroy a Russian warship—without orders or any kind of provocation. All he cared about was that cargo you were carrying. What the hell is that stuff?"

Laz shrugged. "Beats me. We did manage to open the case, which had some pretty ingenious crypto on it, but all it held was twelve test tubes. My best guess was a bio weapon, but someone went to great lengths to obscure where it was coming from. I kept one to make sure I got paid. I was going to give it back, honest."

"And you got paid for the delivery? How much?"

Laz hesitated. "Five million credits."

"Five *million*?" Addison said. "Wow, smuggling pays well."

"That's just it—it doesn't. Not normally. This is the biggest score of my career, by far. Someone wanted this done fast and no questions asked."

Addison nodded. "And now my former four-point-oh skipper has turned into Gollum carrying around his gold ring." She faced Laz. He met her gaze again and it felt ... comfortable. "I think this is going to get worse before it gets better, Laz."

Laz let his eyes roam around the cell.

"Well, you know where to find me, Addie."

Chapter 17

Mars Station

Martin Shasta paused as the lift doors opened, allowing himself a moment of satisfaction at his glorious creation.

They were thirty stories below the surface of Mars, in a bunker that didn't exist on any government document. This is what fifty billion credits looks like, he thought as he surveyed the control room. The space was humming with activity, with technicians calling out to each other and stabbing at their control panels.

"Attention on deck!" someone called, and everyone in the room rose to their feet and fell silent. Martin strode out of the lift, waving his hand as if their gesture of respect meant nothing to him. "As you were, people. As you were."

He wondered who had thought up that little stunt. After thirty-five years in the Fleet, Martin had been forced into retirement, which he fully expected to be a life of boredom. That all changed a week later when the CIA showed up at his door asking him to lead the development of a completely new weapons system, an intelligent laser platform capable of independently killing Russians by the bushel. Even better, as a "black" project, he had unlimited budget; every dime was completely off the books. The only oversight he had to deal with was one Senate committee, but even that was led by Senator Beauregard, or FDB to friends like Martin. His semiannual visits to Washington to brief FDB were more like an excuse to drink heavily and chase women.

But all that had changed overnight. The Swarm. Hell with the Russians, they had a real enemy to fight now. Real aliens, big bad ships, and heavy-duty weapons, just like in the movies. Well, he had just the antidote for that shit. Earth was going to be saved and he, Martin Shasta, the admiral they'd forced out after thirty-five years, was going to be the freaking Hero of the Millennium.

"Status report," he barked at his aide, CJ, a washed-out-looking young man with a terrible nail-biting habit. But the kid had a brain like a computer and never seemed to sleep.

"We'll be ready to launch in ten minutes, Admiral," CJ said with one finger in his mouth. "The safe codes are standing by for you to approve, sir."

Martin slipped into his command chair. He'd modeled the control room after the bridge of a *Constitution*-class warship, with his chair at the center. In truth, this feature was excessive, since they had almost nothing to do once GILD was launched, but he'd been given an unlimited checkbook and he wanted his own command chair.

CJ sidled up next to his chair, pointing at the screen with a wet finger. "All our ships are given a safe code. When they come into contact with a GILD drone for the first time, they transmit the code and that registers their ship with the system. They are locked in as a friendly for a twenty-four-hour period, then they have to reregister."

Martin scanned down the list of ships being given safe codes. All the expected Fleet heavies like *Invincible*, *Constitution*, *Victory*, and *Independence*, then a host of smaller ships, and finally a long list of Russian warships. Russians! The very people we built this system to protect us against were now being given safe codes.

"The Chinese still have not responded?" he said.

CJ shook his head. "No, sir. I heard they walked out on the president when he told them about GILD."

Martin huffed. Stupid bastards; he'd show them what good old American ingenuity could do with a few years and a shit-ton of money. "Sounds good, CJ. What do I need to do?"

CJ's finger left a wet smudge on the screen. "Just put your DNA authorization right here, sir, and we are ready to launch."

Martin pressed his index finger on the spot and waited until the light turned green. CJ nodded. "All ships acknowledge receipt of the codes. We are ready for launch, Admiral."

"Start the countdown," Martin called.

Viewscreens overhead showed the blast doors on the red surface of Mars opening as the countdown sounded. A burst of flame licked out of the opening, then the GILD rocket lifted off. The screens shifted to off-planet mode as the booster punched the rocket into space at double-digit g-forces.

"Three minutes to deployment, sir," called one technician.

"Very well," Martin said, watching the timer.

The GILD system was like a series of stacked pies. At predetermined intervals, a "pie" would deploy by breaking into eight equal pieces, each about half the size of a fighter. After linking with the hive, the GILD units "cleaned" a segment of space by destroying any man-made object bigger than a breadbox that hadn't preregistered with a safe code. The units could act independently or band together like a pack of wolves to attack a larger target.

"First level deploying now."

Martin watched the screen as eight perfect wedges broke off from the mother ship. The room erupted in applause. He sat back in his chair and punched CJ on the arm.

"Perfect," he said.

Martin Shasta crossed his arms. He couldn't wait until those alien ships crossed into *his* space.

Chapter 18

ISS *Invincible* – Bridge

"Standing by for q-jump, sir," Addison said. As XO, it was her responsibility to check and recheck the q-jump coordinates, especially for a high-risk, in-system jump like this.

"Very well, XO," the captain replied. He seemed calmer than he'd been in the admiral's briefing, but Addison could still see the slight bulge in his breast pocket where he was carrying the vial.

"Execute q-jump on my mark," he said. "In three . . . two . . . one . . . mark."

The room shifted and Addison felt her stomach quiver as they made the hop across space-time. She consulted the screen. "Jump successful, Captain." Gnat's ass accurate was more like it, she thought.

"Very well, XO. Sensors, what have we got?"

"Five Swarm ships. Putting them on screen now, sir," said Ensign Proctor.

Addison had seen the video footage, but the new images gave her a fresh spike of fear. The ships were big, much bigger than the *Invincible*.

"The Swarm ships will cross into the GILD system operating area in eighteen minutes, sir," Proctor said.

Comms called out, "Captain, I'm receiving GILD safe codes from Mars. Ready to transmit on your command, sir."

"Very well, Comms." Baltasar swiveled in his chair. "XO, let's close on the enemy ships. I want to try a hail."

Addison tried not to frown. "Sir, our orders are to engage the enemy, not talk to them. The *Eagle* tried that, Captain. The admiral used the words 'unrestricted warfare.'"

Baltasar scowled at her. "XO, if you are unable to do your job, I will have you replaced."

Addison could sense the tension on the bridge. Everyone was staring at their workstations in an effort to avoid hearing the argument between the two most senior officers on the ship.

"Yes, sir," she said. "Helm, intercept course to the lead Swarm ship. Full power."

"Aye-aye, ma'am." The *Invincible* leaped across space. The now-unmistakable sound of the Swarm fleet filled the speakers.

"Turn that noise off, sensors," Addison said.

"Leave it on," Baltasar said. Addison watched her captain listening to the sound, his eyes held in a thousand-yard stare.

"Captain?" Addison said.

The man started in his chair. "Let me see the safe codes, XO."

"Aye-aye, sir." She sent the pending message to the captain's screen. He reviewed it, then nodded. "Very well, XO. Send it."

Addison transmitted the safe codes message to the GILD system.

"GILD system acknowledgment, Captain," said the weapons officer. "They have the *Invincible* registered in their weapons profile."

Baltasar nodded. "Comms, open a channel to the lead alien ship." The room went quiet as the captain pressed a button on his personal screen.

"Alien vessel, this is Captain Jason Baltasar of the ISS *Invincible*. You are about to enter a restricted area. Please respond."

Nothing, just the drone of the Swarm fleet.

Baltasar sat back in his chair. "Bring us to a safe stand-off distance, XO." Addison busied herself with orders to the helm, then turned back toward the captain. He was watching her again. "Time to GILD system engagement, Weapons Officer," he said.

"Three minutes, sir."

Baltasar nodded. "Let's see what the best of mankind can do against Swarm technology."

Addison looked at him sharply. While the rest of the bridge crew, including herself, were battling nerves, Baltasar looked relaxed, almost playful in this moment of ultimate crisis.

"One minute to GILD engagement, sir."

Everyone leaned forward in their seats, eyes locked on the main screen. The Swarm lead ship crossed the line projected on the screen and they waited to see the mass of tiny dots converge on the massive vessel.

Nothing happened.

A collective gasp sounded throughout the bridge.

The comms officer called out, "Incoming message from

Mars Station, Captain."

"On screen." The man on the screen had a florid complexion made even more pronounced by the fact that his face was twisted in rage. "*Invincible*, this is Admiral Martin Shasta—what have you done? The alien ship got access to the safe codes. You were the only vessel that made contact with them."

"Can you reset the system, sir?" Baltasar asked.

Admiral Shasta glared back. "No, you can't just reset the system. It's designed to operate independently. The ships with safe codes are locked in for the next twenty-four hours. They'll be well out of range by then. I promise you, if we make it through this, there will be an investigation. Shasta, out." The screen went dark.

Addison flopped back in her chair, unable to process the disappointment. Already her personal screen was filling with incoming comms as the Fleet tried to regroup from the GILD failure. Out of the corner of her eye, she caught a flicker of movement and saw Ensign Proctor waving frantically at her. Addison crossed the room.

"What is it, Ensign?" The woman's face was ashen. She whispered, pointing to her screen. "I looked at the captain's hail to the Swarm ship. He transmitted the safe codes in his message. It's right here, buried in this side frequency."

Addison felt her stomach fall away. This made no sense. Why would Baltasar turn over secret codes to the enemy?

"Commander Halsey." Baltasar's voice was directly behind her. When she turned, Addison saw he had a weapon pointed at her. "You are under arrest for treason."

Marines surrounded her, pinning her arms to her sides.

"I don't know what game you're playing at, Commander," Baltatsar said harshly, his weapon steady on her chest. "You had the responsibility to transmit the safe codes to the GILD system and somehow they ended up with the enemy." Addison started to protest, but Baltasar cut her off. "Oh, I'm sure you've figured out a way to cover your tracks, Commander, but I'm not buying it."

He nodded at the marines. "Confine her to quarters."

Chapter 19

ISS *Invincible* – Executive Officer's Quarters

Addison paced, then did push-ups until the muscles in her arms failed her. Anything to still her racing brain.

Baltasar was a spy? A decorated Fleet officer, captain of one of the premier warships in the Fleet, was a spy? Not possible. Her brain rejected the idea.

But she had seen the evidence. He had passed the safe codes to the Swarm ships. Proctor had shown her the screen.

Proctor . . . maybe Proctor was the spy? She spent the next thirty minutes trying to figure out how the sensors officer could have manipulated the outgoing transmission to the Swarm ship, but came up with nothing. Besides, Baltasar was the one who insisted they contact the aliens again—against orders.

Baltasar was a spy, that was the only logical answer.

Addison thought about his obsession with the mysterious green vial. There had to be a connection. Was it a weapon of some kind, or maybe an organic storage device that he was tasked to preserve? Her mind reeled.

Stop. Think. Act.

The words of her father echoed in her head. *Don't react, act.*

If she accepted that her captain was a spy, then it was her duty to stop him. Organize a mutiny? That was going to be difficult from her quarters.

A new thought chilled her. What if UEF command didn't realize the *Invincible* was compromised? He'd already attacked and destroyed a Russian warship. She shuddered to think of the damage a *Constitution*-class starship could wreak on an unsuspecting fleet.

She needed to warn the Fleet. Her mind turned over the problem. The idea of hacking the *Invincible*'s comms system by herself didn't seem realistic. Besides, in order to do anything onboard the ship she needed someone she could trust, and right now trust was a commodity in short supply.

It took a full quarter hour before her heart allowed her head to acknowledge the obvious answer: Laz Scollard.

He had a ship and a crew, but could she really trust him?

Beggars can't be choosers. Another choice fatherly saying.

She crossed to the door and punched the intercom. "Corporal, I need to speak to the captain."

The young man's voice came back through the speaker. "Sorry, ma'am, but—"

"Corporal, open this door and talk to me. I'm still the executive officer on this ship!"

She hit him as soon as the door opened, launching her fist at the soft flesh of his throat. He recovered quickly, parrying her next punch, but she had the drop on him. She rang his head against the doorjamb, dragged him inside, and clamped his neck in a sleeper hold. It was over in less than thirty seconds.

Working as fast as she could, she stripped his uniform off and put it on. He was a little thicker in the waist and she was fuller in the hips and chest, but it would pass a cursory inspection. She pushed her hair up into the cap and pulled the brim as low as she dared. Using his handcuffs to bind him, she placed his gagged form into her closet and locked it.

Addison kept her eyes down as she made her way to the brig. She avoided the lifts, worried that if any crew members had a chance to study Corporal Ralston, they would realize they were actually looking at their Executive Officer.

She used the corporal's badge to access the brig area. The marine on duty waved to her, then did a double-take when he saw her name badge. "Hey, you're not—"

He lunged for the alarm, but Addison drew her stunner and fired. She used his own handcuffs to secure him.

Someone had given Laz a rubber ball, and she could hear the rhythm as he bounced it off the floor, the wall, then caught it again. *Pock-pock-slap, pock-pock-slap.* Addison found herself clenching her teeth in frustration. Even in the brig that man could somehow still manage to get special treatment.

When she opened the door to his cell, he didn't look up. "What do you knuckleheads want now?" he said. *Pock-pock-slap.*

"That's the greeting I get?" Addison replied.

Laz's head snapped up. "Addie?" He scanned the uniform. "What are you—"

"No time, Laz. I need that pirate ship of yours to get me off the *Invincible*. Are you in?"

He didn't hesitate. "Of course, Addie."

"Don't call me that."

Laz just grinned. "Based on your terrible disguise, I'm

guessing we're in a hurry, but you need to get my guys out, too."

He walked into the hallway and bellowed, "Topper, Little Dick, Mimi, Gizmo. Sound off!"

Voices yelled back from the very end of the hallway. Addison, working the control panel for the cell doors, finally gave up and opened all the cells. The short black man and the massive bald guy joined them, followed by the dark-haired woman and bearded engineer. "Everyone, this is Addie—"

"Addison," she said. The woman was eyeing her in a way that made Addison want to punch her in the face.

"Whatever," Laz replied. "What's your plan?"

Addison stopped. What was her plan? They needed to get to the *Renegade* on the flight deck, but that was a good ten minutes' travel from where they were now.

"You don't have a plan, do you, Addie?" Laz said.

Addison shook her head.

Laz stared at her for a second. "Alright, here's what we're going to do. Mimi, find a power pack and cross-wire it so it overloads. Little Dick and Topper, find us some weapons and a couple sets of handcuffs. We're going to create a good old-fashioned diversion."

***

They made it halfway to the flight deck before the explosion happened. As the emergency klaxon sounded and the crew raced to their damage control stations, the corporal's communicator badge buzzed. Addison glanced down: *Security alert—Commander Halsey has escaped. Deadly force authorized.*

Deadly force ... Addison unlocked the cuffs on her prisoners. "They're looking for me now and they'll be shooting. No sense in keeping you guys locked up."

Addison's hopes rose as they turned the last corner and she could see the double doors leading onto the flight deck. She stopped.

"The tractor beam," she said. "We'll never get off the ship unless I disable it."

Laz signaled Topper to watch the hallway and Little Dick ran to the flight deck doors. He flashed a thumbs-up.

"Okay, what's your plan, Addie? This is your ship."

"They're coming, Captain," Topper called. He fired a few shots around the corner and received a fusillade in return. "We can't stay here."

Laz watched her. "Addie. Plan. Now."

"Can you fit an X-23 fighter on your cargo deck?"

Laz pulled a face. "Tight fit, but yeah."

"Go, get on the *Renegade* and get out of here. I'll handle the tractor beam. If I make it out, you pick me up."

"And if you don't?"

"Then it's up to you to tell CENTCOM that Captain Baltasar is a spy."

"Addie . . ."

But she was already down the hall and into the pilot's locker room. Addison found her locker and slipped into her flight suit.

***

The flight deck was deserted. Laz and his men had already

boarded the *Renegade* by the time she located an X-23 fighter in a ready status. Her system powered up just as the *Renegade*'s running lights came on. She keyed her radio.

"Control, this is Xray-Bravo-niner-niner, the captain has released the privateer ship *Renegade* with fighter escort." Might as well try the easy way first.

"Bravo-niner-niner, Control, stand by." The operator sounded young, unsure of herself. Just as Addison was hopeful her ploy might work, a new voice came on the net, one with more authority. "Bravo-niner-niner, we're in lockdown. Release denied." As he spoke, a platoon of marines flooded onto the flight deck. Small arms fire filled the air around her. They'd figured out it was her.

Addison switched channels. "Laz, get out of here. I'm right behind you."

"Roger that, Cannonballs." Addison smiled to herself. He remembered her call sign after all these years.

The *Renegade* entered the flight path and gunned her engines. Addison could see movement in the flight control room overlooking the hangar. Time to play her cards. She rose above the parked fighters and pointed the nose of her ship toward the control room. "Control, you have three seconds to evacuate before I start shooting. One ... two ... three." She released a short burst of cannon fire in the far corner of the control room windows. The glass shattered.

"We're clear, Cannonballs," Laz said. "Just waiting on you."

"I'll be right there," Addison said. "Just one more thing to take care of."

Small arms fire raked her underside. Addison spun the fighter in a tight circle so the blast of her engines washed over the marines. They scattered. She nosed closer to the control room. One brave officer was still trying to make it to the tractor beam station.

Addison cursed. She backed the ship away and pointed her cannons at the housing for the power distribution system for the whole flight deck. The fighter stuttered as she raked the nose back and forth across the panel. A small explosion billowed out of the wall and the hangar went dark. Emergency lights flickered on. She'd just killed power to the entire flight deck. Everything was down: lighting, artificial gravity, atmospheric control, blast doors. She hoped to hell the marines on the flight deck had their emergency breathing gear with them.

Addison "Cannonballs" Halsey nosed through the field of floating debris and punched the throttle forward.

Chapter 20

ISS *Warrior*
Lagrange Station Depot

Captain Christian de Santos stared at the screen. "I don't believe it, Admiral," he said flatly.

"Chris, I'm having a hard time myself," Admiral Kilgore replied, "but the *Invincible* transferred the GILD safe codes to the alien ship. It's a fact."

Christian scrubbed his face with both hands. "Ma'am, this is Jason Baltasar we're talking about here. What you are saying is not possible. I know that man like my own brother."

The admiral's face hardened. "Captain de Santos, I didn't call you for a character reference on Captain Baltasar. The GILD system has been compromised and now the only thing that stands between Earth and the Swarm fleet is Lagrange Station."

Lagrange Station was positioned 1.5 million kilometers from the Earth at the L2 point, the point of neutral gravity between Earth and the Sun, a place where zero energy was expended to stay in orbit. The optimum spot for a maintenance depot.

Christian nodded at the screen. "We're evacuating any ships that can get underway and all nonessential personnel, but the *Warrior* is a sitting duck here, ma'am. My weapons systems are fine, but I've only got two engines installed. With two-thirds of my engine room gone I can barely get underway, much less fight."

"Weapons are available?" Kilgore asked.

"Yes, ma'am. I even have a half load-out of torpedoes, since the armory here on Lagrange wasn't equipped to handle that model."

"Do you . . . ?" The admiral's features softened and she stroked her chin. Finally, she turned her full attention back to de Santos. "Captain, I have an idea."

***

Christian de Santos watched the main viewscreen from his command chair. Around him lay the detritus of a ship in the middle of refit—opened panels, pulled wiring harnesses, tools left in the haste of the evacuation—but he ignored it all.

"Remember, Lieutenant, passive sensors only," he said for the third time. The lieutenant manning the sensors panel didn't seem to mind the repeated reminder.

"Confirmed passive only, sir."

"Let's go to full mag, Lieutenant."

"Full magnification, sir."

The five Swarm ships rode in the same arrowhead formation that they'd used when they passed Mars Station. "Show me the *Invincible*." The screen jumped so de Santos could see the UEF warship riding herd about a hundred thousand kilometers off the port side of the enemy ships.

Far enough that Captain Baltasar might be biding his time to make a coordinated attack—or he might be in league with the Swarm. Was it possible that all the communications channels on the *Invincible* were somehow offline?

Not possible, de Santos decided. Something bad had happened on that ship. He only hoped his old friend was okay.

"Time to Swarm contact with Lagrange?" The query came out more harshly than he intended. The few of them that had volunteered for this suicide mission were all on edge. Him barking at people was not going to make it any easier.

"Seventy-three minutes, sir."

"Sorry, Lieutenant," he said after a few minutes. "I didn't mean to snap at you."

"No offense taken, sir. I just . . . well, sir, I just want to say that whatever happens, it's been an honor."

De Santos blinked hard. "Likewise, Lieutenant—and that's all we'll say about that." He swung out of his chair. "I'm going to visit the torpedo bay."

It was a strange feeling to walk through an empty ship. Counting himself and the lieutenant, there were only ten people left onboard: two on the bridge, two in engineering, and six to handle torpedoes. His footsteps echoed in the empty corridors and he whistled to distract himself.

His XO, Commander Joanie Michener, smiled as he came into the torpedo bay. Like the rest of her small team, she had stripped to her T-shirt and her face was red with exertion. "Hey, Skipper, we're all ready for ET down here. All tubes loaded and another full spread standing by, if we have enough time to get them off before . . . whatever happens happens."

She realized she had talked herself into the one topic they'd all rather avoid.

One of the mechanics, a burly woman with wideset eyes and a ready smile, spoke up. "We've been teaching the XO how to move torpedoes manually, sir." She laughed.

"What's your name, sailor?" de Santos asked.

The young woman blushed. "Sorry, sir, it's Torpedoman Third Class Salyer."

De Santos held out his hand. "I'm glad to know you, Salyer. Thanks for being here."

"But sir, this is my torpedo bay. You need me. Nobody knows this place better than I do."

De Santos smiled. "I'm sure you're right, Salyer." He pulled the XO aside. "Joanie, when this goes down, it's going to happen fast. It'll be a miracle if we get the chance to get off a second spread, but do your best."

"I understand, sir. We'll be ready."

De Santos held out his hand. "Good luck, Commander."

She brushed his hand away and hugged him. Then she kissed him on the cheek. "I always wanted to do that," she said. "You can court-martial me later, Christian."

***

The sound of the Swarm was maddening. The lieutenant was on the weapons panel now. They had no need for sensors anymore.

"Time to intercept, Lieutenant?" de Santos said.

"Eight minutes, sir."

Intercept in this case was point-blank range. Their plan

was blindingly simple—or stupid, depending on your point of view. The theory was that the Swarm would not deploy their fighters unless provoked, so the *Warrior* was going to play dead in space dock, systems powered down, acting like they'd been abandoned. When the Swarm passed by, they were going to unload as many torpedoes as possible into the lead ship.

And then deal with the consequences.

"*Warrior*, this is *Invincible*. Come in."

It was Jason Baltasar's voice. De Santos swallowed hard. He and the admiral had discussed this. *Warrior* was to maintain radio silence.

The call came again: "*Warrior*, this is *Invincible* actual. Come in." There was a pause. "Are you there, Christian? It's Jason."

"Shall I answer the hail, sir?"

"No." De Santos wanted nothing more than to reply to the *Invincible*. He had no doubt that with Jason acting in concert, they could take out twice as many of these Swarm bastards. But orders were orders.

"Time to intercept?" the captain said.

"One minute, sir."

De Santos touched his keypad. "It's almost showtime, XO."

"Standing by, sir." Michener's voice was steady.

"Lieutenant, target the lead ship, full spread of torpedoes. Fire!"

The *Warrior* rocked as six torpedoes left the ship.

"Time to impact thirty seconds, Captain."

"XO, reload now!"

De Santos watched the trails of fire cut across the space between them and the alien vessel. The sound of the Swarm vibrated through the hull, making the skin of his arm tingle against the armrest.

Two weapons impacted the Swarm ship, sending out a string of secondary explosions.

"Two hits, sir!" the lieutenant whooped.

"What about the rest of them?" de Santos called.

"I've lost them, sir . . . wait . . . oh my God, look." De Santos stared at the main screen. The other four torpedoes had entered one of the scoops that intel had told them were fighter bays. A massive gout of flame and debris erupted out of the scoop, causing the huge ship to heel hard to starboard. *Take that, you bastards.*

The XO's voice cut through the din of the Swarm noise. "All torpedo tubes reloaded, Captain!"

"Captain, the Swarm fighters are . . . well, swarming, sir."

Even though the lead vessel was heavily damaged, the Swarm was scrambling fighters out of the other ships. Clouds of small craft crisscrossed the viewscreen.

"Let's take this show on the road, Lieutenant. Full forward shields and put us on a collision course with that lead ship." De Santos punched the intercom. "Engineering, give me all the power you've got."

Captain Christian de Santos felt the ship tilt up as they rose toward the alien fleet, masses of enemy fighters nearly obscuring the view of their target. The hull trembled as they began to take a beating from the Swarm forces. He punched the intercom again.

"XO, fire at will."

Chapter 21

SS *Renegade* **– Bridge**

"Addie, wake up. You're going to want to see this."

Addison started awake at Laz's voice. She'd curled up in the first officer's chair, still in her flight suit, determined to watch Laz's every move. But exhaustion had taken over.

She rubbed her face. "What?" Her voice was hoarse.

He sent the image to the main screen. Lagrange Station leapt into view, dwarfed by the five incoming Swarm ships. She saw a flash of light cross between the ships and the station.

"They're fighting back? I thought they'd have evacuated the station."

Laz increased the magnification and Addison saw a massive explosion engulf the lead alien ship. The vessel heeled over, narrowly missing one of its neighbors. A starship shot out of the space dock, releasing another brace of torpedoes as she rose.

"That's *Warrior*," Addison said. Clouds of Swarm fighters engulfed the ship. "Those poor brave bastards," she whispered.

Laz shook his head when she turned toward him. "I know what you're thinking," he said, "and the answer's no. We need to put as much space between us and the bad guys as possible before we contact UEF Command. Once we uncloak to communicate, we're exposed. I don't have the kind of weapons that can stand up to a military vessel. Privateers rely on stealth and speed."

Addison almost made a smart-ass comment about pirates, but she bit her tongue. Whatever Laz's faults—and they were legion—she needed him now. He was her ticket to get back in the fight.

"How long before it's safe to communicate with UEF CENTCOM?"

Laz glanced at his panel. "Give it another hour."

Addison stood and stretched. "Alright. Can I clean up somewhere?"

"Sure." Laz jerked his thumb over his shoulder. "You can use my cabin. Second door on the right. Mimi can lend you some clean clothes if you want."

Addison didn't respond. Somehow, she didn't think Mimi would be all that happy about lending out her clothes.

Laz's cabin was small, but tastefully furnished with thick rugs covering the deck and real wood furniture. She stripped off her uniform and shivered through a quick shower, noticing the water meter next to the faucet. Life on a massive starship had made her forget about how smaller ships like *Renegade* needed to husband their basic resources of air and water.

Dripping wet, she looked around the tiny bathroom. No towel. Cursing her lack of foresight, she yanked open the first drawer she found. Socks, underwear . . . and her picture.

She and Laz were both in uniform, standing on a balcony overlooking a dance floor. Our Ring Dance, she thought. The highlight of completing your third year at Fleet Academy was getting a class ring. It meant you were almost a senior, or first-class midshipman—your last stop to becoming a commissioned officer. She could remember that night like it was yesterday: the smell of the hall, the way she felt when Laz looked at her.

She flipped the picture over. Her own image looked back at her. She was smiling and stray strands of hair flew around her face like a crazy halo. She didn't recognize the place, but the feeling hit like a punch in the stomach. She hadn't laughed like that in . . .

Addison slammed the drawer shut, her vision blurred in anger. *He* left *her*. That's how it happened. He cheated, he left. Game over.

She found a towel in the third drawer and rubbed her body until her skin burned. Then she dressed again in her dirty flight suit and returned to the bridge.

Laz glanced over his shoulder. "Have a seat at the comms station, Addie. Let's give this a try." He punched the intercom. "Topper, Little Dick, man the guns, we're going to uncloak and see what the comms picture looks like out there."

"It's Addison, dammit," she muttered.

"You'll always be Addie to me," Laz replied with a smile.

She threw him a withering gaze. "And you'll never be anything to me."

The grin slid from his features. "What's eating you? I thought we were friends again."

"Twenty years of wishing I was wrong, that's what's eating me. And no, we're not friends."

Laz punched his panel. "I'll keep that in mind. Uncloaking

now. You're on the UEF channel. Feel free to phone home, Commander Halsey."

Addison squared her shoulders and faced the screen. She keyed in her ID code and waited for the system to respond.

"Uh-oh," she heard Laz say.

"Everything okay over there?" What was taking the UEF station so long to respond?

"Looks like we've got company. Chinese frigate, coming in fast." A blast from a pulsed energy weapon flashed blue-green against their shields. "Apparently, they're still unhappy about how the delivery went down."

The UEF security process ground on. "How much time?" she asked.

Laz spoke through gritted teeth. "Ten seconds." The shields absorbed another blast of energy, a stronger one than before.

An operator came onto Addison's screen. "Commander Halsey, I'm connecting you to Fleet Admiral Kilgore now."

"No time," Addison snapped as another blast rocked the ship. "Tell the admiral that Captain Baltasar has been compromised by the Swarm. She can't rely on the *Invincible*." She broke the connection. "Get us out of here, Laz."

One look at his screen and she could tell Laz had held on as long as possible. Maybe too long. The Chinese frigate blazed toward them at full speed, filling the space around them with as much energy as possible.

"He's calling in backup," Laz said, "and trying to light us up with so much energy that the cloak will give us away." He stabbed the intercom. "Topper, how about some return fire, guys?"

"What can I do?" Addison asked.

Laz indicated upwards with his eyes. "We've got a turret gun up top. Be my guest."

Addison hustled up the ladder and dropped into a gunner's seat. The grips for the weapons were worn but operated smoothly. She looped one strap over her arm as she spun the chair.

There. The Chinese frigate looked sleek and deadly with a stylized hull design that terminated in a point. She mashed the trigger, feeling the pulse of the weapon run back through her arms. Another trace lanced out from the side of her ship, scoring a hit on the enemy ship.

"Concentrate on his engines," Laz called over the intercom.

Addison felt the ship turn underneath her as Laz executed a barrel roll. She swung the gun to bear on the Chinese frigate and unleashed a steady stream of weapons fire. The frigate heeled over as the starboard nacelle exploded.

"Cloaking now," Laz said over the intercom. The view outside Addison's gun turret blurred as the cloak took effect. She clambered down from the turret to find the other two gunners in Laz's crew on the bridge.

"What the hell, guys?" Laz yelled. "If we hadn't had the commander onboard, we'd be space dust by now."

"Sorry, Laz," Little Dick said. He hung his massive bald head until his chin touched the mat of hair on his chest. "Gun jammed."

"Yeah, Laz. Gun problems for me, too." Topper said. His black face split into a grin. "Nice shootin', Addison."

"You can call her Commander Halsey, Topper," Laz

snapped. "Now both of you get your asses down there and service those weapons. Next time we might not get so lucky."

When Topper and Little Dick had gone, Laz turned to her. "You really saved our bacon, Addison. Thanks." His face was ashen. "The Chinese are looking for us—me. I don't know what was in that cargo, but they're not going to stop until they have my hide on a wall."

He showed her the tactical screen. Three more Chinese ships were between them and Earth. Addison grimaced. "As soon as we open up a UEF channel, they're going to be on us like white on rice," she said. "We need to let the UEF know what they're dealing with. You got any smuggler tricks left in your bag?"

Laz's face softened. "Are you willing to play outside the rules? For once?"

Addison took in the sly smile, and all she saw was that picture in his drawer. Why had he kept it? He left her, he was the one who walked away from their life together.

"Well? What do you say, Commander?"

He hadn't really changed all that much in twenty years. Still willing to go around the system to get something done. But maybe that's what she needed now.

"What did you have in mind, Laz?"

To Addison's surprise, her smile felt genuine.

Chapter 22

White House, Washington, DC

What President Quentin Chamberlain really wanted was a drink. What he settled for was a stim tablet and a glass of water.

"Show him in," he said to his secretary of state.

He didn't like Oleksiy Ivanov, he didn't trust Oleksiy Ivanov, but the fact remained: he needed Oleksiy Ivanov.

The Russian president filled the doorway with his squat form, a sly smile on his heavy face. He held a briefcase in his left hand, and his right hand shot out in Chamberlain's direction. "Mr. President, I'm so glad you called while I was still in town."

Chamberlain rose slowly, squashing the politician's instinct to rush across the room with an enthusiastic greeting. He needed to make Oleksiy come to him. He needed to keep the upper hand in this meeting. Instead, he bowed his head. "Lucky for me," he said.

If the Russian noticed or cared, he didn't show it. He plodded across the room with all the grace of a geriatric Saint Bernard and crushed Chamberlain's hand in his own. He dropped into the proffered chair, placing the case next to his feet.

Chamberlain nodded to the secretary of state, who had followed the Russian into the room. "That'll be all, Kathy. I'll let you know when I need you."

Kathy frowned. Her boss had gone off script already. Chamberlain narrowed his eyes at her and jerked his head toward the door. They could all go to hell as far as he was concerned. He didn't need a minder.

Oleksiy folded his hands across the bulge of his belly. The man had huge hands—*paws* was a better description, Chamberlain thought.

"Mr. President?" the Russian said in his heavily accented voice.

"Please, it's just the two of us now. No need for titles. Call me Quentin."

"Quentin, then," he said. The *Q* sounded pinched by his accent. "You must call me Oleksiy, then."

Chamberlain smiled. "Oleksiy." He poured a cup of coffee from the tray between them and passed it to the Russian. The man dragged the sugar bowl toward him and scooped in three heaping spoonfuls. His vigorous stirring was the only sound in the room. Chamberlain poured a cup for himself, hoisting it toward Ivanov in salute.

"Can't stand sugar myself," he said. "Black and bitter for me. Just like my outlook on the future."

It took a moment for Ivanov to get the joke. He laughed, a loud, booming noise that sounded like a sea lion in heat. "This too shall pass," he said.

Chamberlain tried to contain his surprise. "I'm surprised to hear you say that, Oleksiy. For my part, I was disappointed by our meeting with the Chinese and the Caliphate. They seemed to have a different view of the alien threat."

Ivanov waved his hand, coffee slopping into the saucer. "The Chinese with pretty ships. Who can tell what they are thinking? And the Caliphate . . ." He shrugged. "No ships to speak of, so no big loss for us, right?"

Chamberlain focused on his coffee. A superficial assessment, but not incorrect. He sighed. "There's another issue, Oleksiy."

Ivanov stopped stirring his coffee. "Oh?"

Chamberlain watched the Russian's eyes as he spoke. "I have reason to believe the aliens have infiltrated our ranks."

Ivanov's gaze froze. He doesn't know, Chamberlain thought.

"Oh," the Russian said again. "How do you mean, Quentin?"

"I mean they have moles among us. Spies, people who have been turned."

"Such as?"

Chamberlain hesitated. Once he told the Russian, it was all over. They were either in it together or the Russian would use the information to destroy him.

"One of our starship captains is a spy."

Ivanov didn't even bother to try to hide his shock. His mouth gaped open, revealing a lifetime of poor dental work. "The *Invincible*?"

Chamberlain nodded.

Ivanov shook his head. "A *Constitution*-class starship captain. Amazing." He resumed stirring his coffee. "Do you know how it happened?"

Chamberlain kept his chin up. "Not yet, but we'll figure it out."

Ivanov grunted. The scraping of the man's spoon was starting to get on Chamberlain's nerves. He held up the coffee pot. "More coffee, Oleksiy?"

The Russian set down his cup and saucer with a clatter of china. "We need to make a pact, Quentin."

"Pardon?"

To his surprise, the Russian stood up and began pacing the room. He settled into a racetrack pattern beneath a portrait of George Washington. "This is worse than I thought, Quentin. Your revelation confirms certain . . . information we have been receiving from assets in China. They report the Chinese Premier has been acting strangely, not in keeping with the goals of the Party. Some have suggested he may be compromised."

Compromised. That was the same word used to describe Captain Baltasar. He smiled at the Russian. "Continue, Oleksiy."

"If this Swarm—as you call them—are capable of compromising a UEF starship captain, why not the Chinese Premier?" He paused in his pacing. "Why not you or I?"

Why not indeed? Chamberlain thought.

"We need to combine forces," Ivanov continued. "A mutual defense pact against the alien threat. If they have access to a starship captain, then they have access to your tactics, battle plans, and so on?" He cocked an eyebrow at Chamberlain, who nodded.

"Exactly!" Ivanov smacked his fist into an open palm, the sound echoing in the room. "So we must throw them out. Do the unexpected. Do you have any joint battle plans for an alliance between Russia and the UEF?"

Chamberlain shook his head.

"Neither do we, so no one can compromise us, right?"

Chamberlain's head ached with the possibilities, but the Russian's proposal had the ring of logic to it. He stood. "Right."

Ivanov crossed the room and crushed Chamberlain's hand in his bearlike grip. "Together we will destroy the alien force, then the Chinese."

"Together," Chamberlain repeated.

Chapter 23

SS *Renegade* **– Airlock**
Space debris around Lagrange Station

The ISS *Warrior* had been cleaved in two. Addison wouldn't have believed the hull of a *Constitution*-class starship could be cut in half like that if she hadn't seen it for herself. It had taken some convincing to get Laz to backtrack to Lagrange Station so she could survey the Swarm ship. Now she was starting to wonder if this was really a good idea after all. This place was a graveyard.

"Life signs on the *Warrior*?" she whispered.

"Negative," Mimi replied from the sensors station. "Nothing human, anyway. Aliens? Your guess is as good as mine."

They watched a Swarm fighter float by, undamaged but seemingly unmanned. Addison stepped behind Laz. "How close can you get me to the Swarm wreckage?"

Laz pulled a face. "With the cloak engaged I can probably navigate around most of this. It would help if I knew what you were looking for."

"I'm not sure." Addison chewed her lip. "Find the biggest

undamaged part of the alien ship. I want to go aboard."

The rest of the *Renegade* crew looked at her. "You want to go aboard?" Laz said. "What if they're nine-foot-tall lizards with sharp teeth that can live in space?"

"Then that would be a good thing for CENTCOM to know, wouldn't it?"

Laz blew out a breath. "In order for us to get you off the ship, I'll need to drop the cloak. That's risky."

Addison looked at the screen full of massive chunks of shattered spaceship—human and alien. "I think we can blend in here, don't you?"

Laz shrugged.

***

As she stood in the airlock, leashed to a small space scooter, Addison had second thoughts. She wasn't trained to survey an alien vessel. What did she hope to find?

Addison turned and gave Topper and Little Dick, also dressed in pressure suits, a thumbs-up. They exchanged unenthusiastic glances. "Bridge, this is the survey team, we're ready to go in 'Lock One."

"We're not that formal here, Commander." Laz's voice dripped with sarcasm. He had wanted to go with her, but Addison refused. He needed to stay to make sure they were able to contact UEF. That was her stated reason, but the real reason was that she didn't trust the rest of his crew not to leave her, especially Mimi. Addison had clearly interrupted some relationship—maybe financial, maybe romantic, maybe both—between Mimi and Laz. The other woman was not happy about it and not afraid to let her feelings show.

Good riddance. Mimi could have him if she wanted him.

"Alright, Laz, let's do this," she said into her mike.

"Dropping cloak," Laz replied. "Opening 'Lock One." The exterior door yawned open, inducing the sense of vertigo she always felt when she started a spacewalk. She focused on the sound of her own breathing to calm her nerves.

"Here we go, Commander," Topper said in his deep voice. Her line went taut as the man gunned the scooter out of the airlock.

The piece of Swarm wreckage was massive, at least three times the size of *Renegade*. She directed Topper to do a slow external survey of the debris. It appeared this piece must have been near the bow of the Swarm ship. They passed one of the laser emplacements, an enormous dish, easily twice the size of any energy weapon the UEF possessed. She thought about the hull of the *Warrior*, cleaved in half. The amount of focused energy required to do that kind of damage . . .

"There's no guns," Little Dick said. She looked over at him, trailing along on his tether, arms wrapped around his own pulse rifle.

"What?" Addison said.

"No point defenses," Topper said. "No laser cannons, no rail guns, nothing."

"Just giant lasers," Addison finished for him. "And lots of fighters."

"And really, really good armor," Little Dick said. They swung closer to view the exterior plating on the ship: a series of overlapping plates, like scales.

"Let's go inside," Addison said.

Laz's voice interrupted her thoughts. "Not a good idea, Commander. You've gotten great intel. Let's call it a day."

She pointed at a gaping hole in the interior of the ship. "Anchor there, Topper."

If it was possible to drive a space scooter reluctantly, Topper managed it. Little Dick floated forward to clamp the anchor to the structure. Addison detached herself and pushed toward the wreckage. She energized her mag boots, feeling the footwear grip the surface.

"We're in, Laz." She focused her light into what looked like a hallway. "Well, I can report they are not nine feet tall. More like four feet, maybe." The passageway was definitely built to accommodate much shorter statured beings than the average human. Addison reckoned if she hunched over, she could make it.

"Yeah, well maybe the nine-foot lizards crawl instead of walk upright," Laz retorted. Addison saw her two companions exchange worried glances again.

"I'm going in," she said.

"Topper, you go with her," Laz said.

"Look, boss, I don't—"

"Do it!"

Addison started walking down the alien passageway without waiting for him. Topper's helmet light appeared behind her. The side passage connected to a main hallway that was wider, but not any taller. Every room they looked in was empty of bodies; the only evidence that there had been beings there at all was a sticky gray mess that clung to the panels. Did the aliens evaporate when exposed to a vacuum?

They entered a side room. Addison scanned the dead

panels, covered in hundreds of geometric shapes. It reminded her vaguely of their own flight control room, just scaled up to account for thousands of fighters instead of dozens. She recorded everything, then stepped back into the main hallway. Her back was killing her from walking hunched over and her thigh muscles burned.

"Addison, you about done over there? I'm picking up some Chinese ships on long-range scanners."

"A few more minutes," she replied, avoiding Topper's angry gaze by turning deeper into the ship. The hallway dead-ended at a large circular object that spanned four levels of the interior. Addison was able to stand up and stretch out her back as she looked around. In fact, *all* hallways dead-ended at the circular object. Control room?

The curved walls of the sphere seemed to be formed from a different material than the rest of the ship. Polished to the point where she could see her own reflection, kind of like a cross between glass and steel. Addison pointed the handheld sensor at the wall, but it came back with a null reading. "Damn thing," she muttered.

"Addison, you guys about done over there?" Laz's voice crackled in her ear. "If you haven't found the lizards by now, they probably all abandoned ship."

"Very funny. I got a strange reading from this wall. I think it's a new element."

"Great, we'll call it Addisonium. Will you just leave now? Please?"

Addison ignored him. She stalked around the exterior of the sphere, thankful for the headroom but very aware of the darkness around her. She stopped at a set of double doors covered in hieroglyphics, made shadowy by her helmet light. "Let's open it," she said.

"Are you nuts?" Topper said. "We have no idea what's in there."

But Addison had already pulled the all-purpose tool from her belt and was working the blade into the central seam in the doors. "Help me, Topper," she said through gritted teeth. The shorter man knelt next to her with his own tool. Together they levered the doors apart. Addison was surprised when a stream of atmosphere shot out past them. The room had still been pressurized, which meant . . .

She scrambled back, pulling out her sidearm. Topper had done the same. With her weapon trained on the doorway, Addison advanced in small steps, Laz's nine-foot dragons in the back of her mind.

The room was empty, but it still had power because the panels glowed. She swung her weapon slowly across the room, taking it all in. Definitely not a control room. Instead, it seemed more like a . . . *chapel* was the only word that came to mind. She couldn't shake the feeling that the chamber seemed holy.

The space was divided into seven quadrants, each with a corresponding star chart and separate panel with raised hieroglyphics, reminding Addison of stained glass windows in an old-fashioned church. She stopped at the nearest one, sucking in a breath. At the center of the star chart was a nine-planet solar system with the third planet highlighted in bright orange. *Earth.* She studied the chart, trying to make sense of the markings. It dawned on her slowly: she was looking at a map of the human population across the galaxy.

She swung her attention to the other sectors. The star charts were unfamiliar to her, but they had the same type of highlighted markings. Other races?

"Commander, look," Topper said. He was pointing at the center of the room where all the seven sections of the room met in a pyramid shape. The seven-sided structure pulsed with energy. The entire central display was covered in a thick layer of the same gray goo they'd seen in smaller quantities all around the ship, and a nine-digit hieroglyphic hologram floated in the air above the pyramid. One digit changed in a regular pattern.

"What is that?" she whispered.

"I dunno," Topper said. "A clock? Look, let's bugger out of here, Commander. This place gives me the willies."

"A clock . . . that's an interesting idea—"

The floor trembled under her feet. She looked at Topper, but he was already moving toward the door. Addison followed as fast as she could.

"What going on over there?" Laz said, concern in his voice. "We just saw an energy spike and part of the wreckage blew out."

"We found something," Addison said from outside the chamber. The floor rumbled again and the deck below them fell away. Topper scrambled down the hallway, back the way they'd come.

Addison waited long enough to see the circular chamber fire off thrusters and drop out of sight. Then she followed Topper's retreating lights.

Chapter 24

SS *Renegade* – Bridge

The Swarm ignored Lunar Base. Addison watched the four remaining Swarm vessels enter high orbit around Earth, escorted by *Invincible*. Captain Baltasar apparently found no need to disguise his alignment with the alien race any longer.

"How good is your cloak against the Swarm technology?" she asked. Her whole body ached from the extra g's they'd pulled as they raced in from Lagrange.

Laz shrugged. "As far we can tell, as good as against UEF sensors. If you flood the area around us with background radiation, we look like a hole in space. As long as no one is shooting at us we should be fine, Commander."

Addison grunted. Although he spoke her title without any trace of irony, it still made her uncomfortable. Maybe she'd been too harsh on him earlier. No time for that now, she thought.

"When am I going to hear about your super-secret comms channel?"

He shrugged again. "These things take time."

Time. The one thing they didn't have anymore.

With its blue oceans and swirling cloud patterns, she'd always enjoyed the view of Earth from space, but the line of Swarm ships marred the peacefulness of the scene. The fact that the alien column of ships was led by one of their own made the picture all the more jarring.

"Any sign of the Fleet?" she asked Laz.

He pointed to his screen. "Here comes the armada."

Addison looked over his shoulder at the fleet of ships massing on the far side of the moon. *Armada* was the right word for it. "Are those Russian warships?" she asked.

Laz nodded. "We're looking at a who's who of the Jane's Ships of the Fleet," he said, referring to a common resource they'd both studied at the Academy. In addition to the *Constitution*, there was the *Independence* and the *Victory*, both carriers like the *Constitution*, as well as the *Tighe*, *Flint*, *Pittsburgh*, and a number of smaller ships. She scanned the Russian contingent: *Vladivostok*, *Brezhnev*, and *Murmansk* were all heavy cruisers with plenty of firepower.

"Looks like the Russians are joining forces with the UEF," she said with a hollow laugh. "Now we know this is serious."

"No Chinese," Laz observed.

Addison studied the lineup. "We know it takes a ton of firepower to knock out one of those Swarm ships. Our lasers are pretty much ineffective unless you can punch through their hull with the rail guns first. Nukes work, but you need to be right on top of them . . . as far as fighters go, if the other four alien ships carry the same fighter contingent as the lead ship, we're in trouble. They'll eat our smaller ships alive. And I'm sure Baltasar will tell them everything there is to know about UEF defenses—"

"What is going on down there?" Laz was pointing out the windows toward the orbiting alien battle group.

The Swarm vessels were forming an arrowhead configuration again with *Invincible* in the lead position. She watched them disappear over the horizon as they made another orbit of Earth.

A few minutes later, they came into view again, passing over the Atlantic Ocean. The starboard ship belched out a ball of fire as they crossed the East Coast of North America.

She pounded Laz on the shoulder. "Where is it headed?" The weapon transited the atmosphere, leaving a trail of vapor and smoke in its wake.

"Cleveland," Laz said finally. "It's going to land on Cleveland."

Addison could only imagine what it looked like from the earth's surface. A ball of fire streaking across the sky, the sonic boom shattering windows as it passed overhead, the terror . . .

"Three seconds to impact." Laz's voice was raspy with emotion.

The detonation created a horribly beautiful mushroom cloud of dusty brown and brilliant yellow, lit from within by furious flashes of lightning.

The sound of the Swarm swelled in the ship's speakers. Suddenly, it stopped and an open hail blanketed all frequencies. Laz looked up at her. Addison nodded. "Answer it," she whispered.

Captain Jason Baltasar's head and shoulders filled the screen. His eyes glittered with emotion and he smiled thinly.

"Greetings, People of Earth. I have the honor to speak on behalf of an alien race, the ones you call the Swarm. Your warships have been unable to stop us. We have given you a small demonstration of our destructive might." He paused to flash a picture of the devastation that had once been Cleveland. "We demand unconditional surrender. All races, all people. No exceptions, no bargaining. You have one hour to decide. If you do not comply, we will destroy another city."

The screen went blank. The drone of the Swarm noise rose again.

Topper and Little Dick had come up behind Addison and Laz on the bridge. Tear tracks creased the dark skin of Topper's cheeks.

"What are we gonna do?" Little Dick asked.

Laz said nothing. He just stared at the blank screen.

"We have to do something," Addison said.

"Great intentions, Commander, but I think we need more of a plan than that." Laz's tone was sharp with sarcasm.

Addison snapped back, "I can't help but think that the cargo you were carrying has something to do with this, Lazarus."

"Of course, it's *my* fault. It's always my fault, isn't it, Addie?" Laz launched out of his chair, taking a stance over Addison that put his face right in hers. "Blame me. You've been doing it for twenty years, why stop now?"

"Oh, that's rich, coming from you. At least I didn't run away like a little bitch—"

"Stop it!" Topper shouted, stepping between them. "You two want to do something, why not stop that guy? The captain?"

Addison didn't bother wiping the tears out of her eyes. There was nothing in the world she'd enjoy more than stopping Baltasar, but to do that they'd need to—

"That's it." Addison threw her arms around Topper. "If we can retake the *Invincible*, that makes us an even match against the Swarm. Well, more even, anyway."

"You have a plan?" Laz raised his eyebrows. The furious redness had left his cheeks.

"I have a plan." Addison bent over the screen and touched one of the UEF warships. The screen expanded to show the ISS *Victory*. "Set an intercept course for her." She faced Laz. She wanted to say she was sorry, but the words wouldn't come out. Instead, she said, "Now would be a good time for that super-secret comms channel with UEF CENTCOM."

Laz's voice had lost its fire. "Aye-aye, ma'am."

Chapter 25

SS *Renegade* – Flight Deck

Little Dick helped her into the cockpit of her fighter and handed her helmet up. "Good luck, Commander," he said.

"Little Dick, you can call me Addison."

A slow smile spread across his broad face. "I like that name." He frowned. "What about Captain Laz?"

"He can call me Commander," she said.

"He likes you," Little Dick replied. "I can tell."

"Yeah, well, once upon a time I liked him, too." She slammed her helmet down on her head. "But that was a long time ago."

The strobe overhead started to flash yellow, indicating a pending depressurization. "You'd best get going, Little Dick."

"Good luck, Addison." He tucked the ladder under his arm and plodded to the door.

"Alright, Commander," said Laz, "we're going to slow down and poop you right out the back. Hopefully, the uncloaking will be so quick that no one even notices."

"Poop, huh? That's what you think of me?"

Laz chuckled. "Poor choice of words, I guess. Look,

Commander, if this doesn't work out, we might not get to talk again, so I just want to say—"

"Save it, Laz. This is going to work." It was a lie and they both knew it.

"Even so," he began.

"Stow it and give me a countdown."

The strobe overhead turned red and the airlock doors opened to reveal a star-studded background. Her panel was green. Laz's voice was low and confident in her ears, just like the old days.

"Launch in three . . . two . . . one . . . GO."

She punched the throttle and shot out into space.

***

The transit toward the inbound fleet was unnervingly uneventful. She engaged the autopilot and allowed her mind to relax. The stars were sharp and bright against the darkness, like diamonds on velvet; the only sound was her own breathing. In this moment of beauty, she could almost forget the existential threat that orbited her home planet.

Her panel blinked as she crossed the sensor line for the Fleet. Addison keyed her mike. "ISS *Victory*, this is *Invincible* fighter Xray-bravo-niner-niner. Request permission to land." She turned on her ID beacon.

"Fighter Xray-bravo-niner-niner, stand by."

Her panel lit up as their fire-control systems targeted her. She keyed her mike again. "*Victory*, this is Commander Addison Halsey, requesting permission to land. Over."

"Fighter Xray-bravo-niner-niner, permission granted.

Starboard fighter bay, Commander. Stand by for auto-recovery lock-on."

"Acknowledge auto-recovery. Niner-niner, out."

Addison steered into the flight lane for the correct fighter bay and waited for the automatic recovery system to take control of her craft. She never liked automatic systems, but in this case it was the best way to show she was not a threat. She crossed her arms as the ship flew past the point-defense rapid-pulse ordnance (RPO) guns, any one of which could rip her ship apart in a matter of seconds.

Her fighter passed through the field generator that kept the flight deck at atmosphere and she squinted as light flooded through her canopy. The auto-recovery was guiding her craft onto a cleared deck. A full squad of armed marines waited for her.

The ship settled with a slight bump and the marines ringed her fighter. Addison opened the canopy and raised her hands, calling out, "I'm coming out. Unarmed."

She stood slowly, waiting while a flight tech rolled a ladder into place and scuttled away. Addison climbed down the ladder carefully. When her boots touched the flight deck she turned around, arms still raised. "I need to speak with Commander Samantha Avery."

A marine lieutenant stepped up. "She's waiting for you, ma'am, but I'm going to have to ask that you take off your flight gear out here and change into this." He tossed a hospital gown at her.

"You're serious?"

"Yes, ma'am. There's a concern that you're some kind of an alien and this is one way to know for sure."

"By me getting naked in front of a whole squad of marines?"

To his credit, the lieutenant blushed. "I don't make the rules, ma'am." He motioned at the gown with the muzzle of his rifle. "Please."

Addison stripped off her flight suit until she was standing in her underwear, bra, and T-shirt. "Is this good enough?"

The lieutenant blushed again, shaking his head. "Sorry, ma'am."

Addison bristled as she pulled her T-shirt over her head. "Get a good look, boys. The show won't last long."

She put her arms through the hospital gown and held the back together. "Shall we proceed, Lieutenant?"

"Follow me, ma'am," he said, leading the way toward a personnel door. As Addison followed, the marines ringed her. The lieutenant keyed open the door and stepped back.

After Addison entered, the door clanged shut and she heard a magnetic lock slam into place. Behind a heavy glass wall sat a woman her own age with thick brown hair and a frown on her face.

"Sam," Addison said. "Am I glad to see you."

"I wish I could say the same, Addison." Her frown deepened. "You've got some explaining to do."

Chapter 26

ISS *Victory* – Medical Quarantine Area

Her first-level debrief with Commander Sam Avery had gone well enough that Addison was sent through decontamination and given a uniform—along with a pair of marine guards and strict orders not to speak about the *Invincible* to anyone on board the *Victory*.

"We've found evidence of Swarm moles throughout the ranks of government and the military," Sam told her. "In almost every case, they're exemplary performers who suddenly get a personality transplant."

"That's exactly what happened to Captain Baltasar," Addison said. "He just blasted across Russian-controlled space and attacked the *Leningrad*. No warning, no orders. He just snapped."

Sam eyed her. "Our best guess is that it's a virus of some kind, but we don't know how it's transmitted." She nodded at the red scrapes on the back of Addison's hands where the decon droid had gotten a little rough. "You're clean, by the way —as far as we can tell."

Addison's foot tapped a rapid tattoo on the deck. "What's

the Fleet status, Sam? Are we ready to launch a counterattack?"

"You know I can't discuss that with you, Addison. Yes, you're clean, but . . ."

Addison took a deep breath. "We've known each other for how long, Sam? You were my plebe-year roommate, for God's sake. If there's any person in the universe who knows me, it's you."

"There's nothing I can do, Addison. The admiral has a standing order out. And before you tell me to call the admiral, we are on complete comms lockdown until the actual moment of battle."

Addison leaped to her feet, pacing the length of the conference room. Sam watched her with slitted eyes. "I didn't come here to turn myself in, Sam. I have a plan to get back in the fight."

"You're on the sidelines for this one, Addison. Sorry."

"No!" Addison slammed both fists on the table. The marine guard at the door peered in the glass, but Sam waved him away. Addison caught her lip in her teeth and pressed down. Maybe she was crazy after all. She slid back into her seat, placing both palms flat on the table.

"Look—what if I had a way to recapture the *Invincible*?"

Sam eyed her warily. "If we could take the *Invincible* out of the fight, that would even the odds for us. Even with the Russians on our side, we're not feeling great about our prospects."

Addison shook her head. "I'm not talking about taking the *Invincible* out of commission, I want to retake her. Put her back in the fight. On our side."

"I'm listening."

Addison resisted the urge to pace again. She lowered her voice, forcing herself to talk slower. "What if we had a ship that could land on the *Invincible* flight deck with a platoon of marines?"

Sam frowned. "You mean like a troop carrier? Those things are tin cans. They'd be shot to pieces the moment the *Invincible* picked them up on sensors. Suicide mission."

"Not if the ship was cloaked," Addison said carefully.

"The only country with cloaking technology is the Caliphate, and they don't have any warships." Sam's frown cleared. "That's how you got here! You came in a cloaked ship. That's why we didn't pick you up on sensors until the last minute."

Addison nodded.

"So you have access to a cloaked ship? One you can use for this cockamamie plan of yours?"

Addison nodded again.

Now it was Sam's turn to pace. "That could work, Addison. If we used the *Victory* to get you as close as possible and gave you a small fighter escort, it's feasible for you to shoot your way onto the *Invincible*." She spun on her heel. "I can sell that to the captain, I think."

Addison shifted in her seat. "Well, there's one tiny problem."

"What?"

Addison told her.

"Are you out of your flipping mind, Addison? Lazarus freakin' Scollard? That lying scumbag got thrown out of Fleet Academy and broke your heart to boot. *He's* part of the plan?"

"He's . . . changed."

Sam snorted. "No, you're an idiot. I can't believe—"

"He has the ship we need, Sam."

"So we take it from him and do the plan ourselves."

"If Laz isn't part of the plan, then you can count me out." Why the hell had she said that? Still, that was no idle threat; they needed her for this to work. Every *Constitution*-class ship had slight idiosyncrasies in design and layout. As the person most familiar with the *Invincible*, she would be a key part of the boarding party.

"You're serious?" Sam said.

"I'm serious."

Sam shrugged. "It's a good plan, despite your lousy judge of character. If you want to trust your life to that lying sack of crap, then it's your funeral. I'll take it to the Old Man."

Chapter 27

White House, Washington, DC

It was difficult for President Quentin Chamberlain to take his eyes off the screen. Cleveland—or the fifty-mile radius that used to be Cleveland—was nothing but a smoking crater of radioactivity.

"Why did they choose Cleveland?" he asked.

The bustle of activity in the Situation Room halted momentarily as the assembly of politicians and military leaders focused on his question.

"I'm not sure, sir," ventured his secretary of state. "I'm not sure it matters."

Chamberlain tore his eyes away from the screen. "Okay, maybe the city doesn't matter"—he winced at his own word choice—"but why not DC or New York or San Francisco? Why Cleveland?"

"They just bombed Saint Petersburg!" one of the generals called out. A new satellite image flashed onto the screen. Not that it mattered to Chamberlain; if you've seen one nuked city, you've seen them all.

"So now the Russians are in it, too," the secretary of state muttered.

"What about China?" Chamberlain asked, thinking about Ivanov's claim that the premier of the People's Republic of China was a Swarm agent.

"Nothing yet, sir," replied one of the Joint Chiefs.

"Mr. President, we're on the clock with the aliens," said State. "What is our answer?"

"How far away is the Fleet?" Chamberlain asked.

"Ninety minutes, sir."

So there it was: give up without even a fight or condemn another American city—maybe the one he was sitting in—to annihilation.

"Options," he said to the table.

"We need to get you to a safe location, sir. If they decide to hit Washington . . ."

"Send the Vice President," Chamberlain replied.

"We've already moved him to Recluse One, sir," said the Secret Service representative, referring to the top-secret command bunker in Appalachia.

"They just bombed Milan," said another general. Chamberlain didn't bother to look at the screen this time.

"Admiral," he said, "talk to me about the precautions we're taking to make sure we don't have a repeat of the Baltasar incident."

"Sir, our working theory is that we're dealing with a virus or parasite that has the ability to rework the personality of the host."

"So we think Captain Baltasar was infected recently?"

"We don't know that, sir."

"But he seems to be able to communicate with the Swarm

—something which we seem unable to do. How is that possible?"

"We don't know that either, sir."

"So what you're telling me is that any one of you could be a Swarm agent and we have no way of knowing?"

To her credit, the admiral didn't avoid his gaze. "Yes, sir."

Chamberlain closed his eyes. He had to face the facts: there were no good options.

"Mr. President?"

He opened his eyes to see his personal secretary looking down on him.

"Mr. President, Masoud el-Hashem is waiting to see you."

"The Caliphate leader wants to see me? Now? Did he say why?"

"He says he has a message for you, sir."

The head of the Secret Service started to get up. "I'll handle this, sir. We can't allow him to—"

Chamberlain waved him down. "Show him into the Roosevelt Room. I'll see him there."

***

El-Hashem bowed when Chamberlain entered the room. "I appreciate your attention in this time of crisis, Mr. President. My deepest condolences on the loss of your citizens."

Chamberlain kept the table between them and did not offer to shake hands. "Mr. el-Hashem, thank you, but I must insist we get down to business. I assume you are here to offer your assistance in the fight against the Swarm."

"I am here to deliver a message, Mr. President."

Chamberlain sat down on the edge of his seat. How could the man be so calm at a time like this? "Well, get on with it, then."

El-Hashem nodded at the secretary of state, who was about to take the chair next to Chamberlain. "The message is for you alone, Mr. President. One cannot be too careful at a time like this."

Chamberlain nodded to State, who left the room.

"We're alone now. Please, let's move this along."

El-Hashem nodded. "One of your officers escaped from the *Invincible*. The Executive Officer, Commander Addison Halsey."

"Yes, yes, we know that. We got a short message from her, but we've been unable to contact her since."

The man gave Chamberlain a patient smile. "That is why I am here. Commander Halsey is a very resourceful officer. She has a plan to retake the *Invincible*, but she requires your help."

Chamberlain leaned forward in his seat. "I'm listening."

El-Hashem smiled again. "Please do not be alarmed by what I am about to share with you, Mr. President." He tapped the side of his temple and a hologram projected out of his left eye. "Meet Captain Lazarus Scollard, of the Caliphate ship *Renegade*."

Chamberlain studied the man before him. Late-thirties, with dark hair and a scruffy beard, Captain Scollard looked like someone who'd spent the previous night drinking.

El-Hashem spoke. "We're using Caliphate technology to effect a person-to-person link. Our conversation is based on a long-dead Persian dialect. Even if the Swarm or anyone else could hack the link, there's no way they could translate what we're saying. Do you understand, sir?"

Chamberlain nodded.

The man in the hologram spoke: "I'm contacting you on behalf of Commander Halsey. She's aboard the *Victory* now and she has a plan to retake the *Invincible*."

"I'm listening."

"She's going to need two things to pull this off, sir. Firstly, she's needs the full cooperation of the *Victory*. I have a coded message for you to send to the captain of the *Victory* to ensure she gets the support she requires."

Chamberlain raised his eyebrows. "That's something I can do. What's the second thing?"

"She needs time, sir."

***

Five minutes later, the President was back in the Situation Room. He slid into his chair and squared his shoulders. "Put Captain Baltasar on the screen, please."

Baltasar appeared a few seconds later. His eyes gleamed and he smiled slyly. "Right on time, Mr. President. Your new masters appreciate your punctuality."

"Our answer is no," Chamberlain interrupted.

Baltasar's head snapped up. Glaring at the screen, he said, "That is not an acceptable answer, Chamberlain. We will annihilate one city every hour until you comply."

"We will destroy you," Chamberlain shot back.

Baltasar shook his head. "You will suffer a fool's death, Chamberlain." The screen went black.

"The Swarm is dropping another weapon, sir." The secretary of state's face was stony.

Chamberlain ignored her. "Admiral, I want you to transmit a message to the Fleet."

Kilgore frowned. "Yes, sir. We've instructed them to maintain comms security, but we can contact them if you wish. What do you want to say?"

"Two words, Admiral: *high jinks*."

Chapter 28

ISS *Victory* – Captain's Ready Room

Captain Sean Rimaud looked more like a concert pianist or a librarian than a starship captain. He surveyed Addison with undisguised distaste.

"I should say up front that the only reason you're even talking to me is because of Commander Avery. I respect her too much to say no, but I am . . . skeptical, to say the least." He stroked his chin with long, slender fingers as he spoke.

Sam had warned her, Addison thought. Still, her chance of even getting to speak with any other starship captain was next to nil. The same military bureaucracy that had once given structure to her life she now saw as an impediment to making a difference in the upcoming battle. One thing she knew for sure: if they stuck to standard UEF battle tactics, Baltasar would eat them alive.

"Thank you, Captain. I appreciate your open mind on this plan."

Rimaud sniffed. "*Plan* is a bit of a stretch, wouldn't you say, Commander? You want to board a *Constitution*-class starship that is in enemy hands and retake it with a platoon of my marines? How do you know that Baltasar hasn't infected the entire crew?"

"I don't, sir. But at the least we can surprise him, right? Catch him off guard? Surely that's worth something."

Rimaud spun in his chair. "Then there's the matter of your accomplice. Lazarus Scollard, an Academy washout—for an honor violation, no less. You trust your life with this man, Commander?"

"I do, sir."

"Well, I don't." He shook his head. "My answer is no, Commander. I'm not going to risk my ship and crew on some half-baked idea that will lead to a lot of men getting killed—including you, I might add."

"I'm willing to take that chance, Captain."

"Well, I'm not!" Rimaud shouted back. He lurched to his feet, walking to the window.

Addison switched tactics. "What about presidential authority, sir?"

Rimaud's reflection in the window laughed at her. "We are under comms lockdown by the order of the President. If you can get the President to violate his own order and send me your super-secret password, then I'm your man, Commander."

It took another six minutes for Captain Rimaud to become "her man."

Rimaud stared at the tablet, then back at Sam Avery. "You're sure this is valid, XO?"

"Yes, sir. We verified it's from DC with the President's electronic signature on it."

Rimaud stood and extended his hand. "Welcome aboard, Commander Halsey. My ship is at your disposal."

***

Laz walked down the ramp from the rear of the *Renegade*.

"I don't believe it," Sam whispered to Addison. "I figured he'd be dead by now." She leveled her gaze at her friend. "Probably shot dead by a jilted lover."

Laz approached the pair tentatively. He nodded at Sam. "You made commander, Sam. Congrats." He looked at Addison. "You okay?"

"Thanks to you," she said.

"Like I said, we in the Caliphate have our methods. The Supreme Leader is the real hero here. He met with the President personally."

Sam interrupted as a marine lieutenant approached them. "We've got less than an hour to make this all happen, you two. Let's get started. This is Lieutenant Ojambe—I believe you've met him already, Addison."

"It's good to see you again, ma'am," the marine said with a wink. "In uniform."

Addison blushed. "Thank you, Lieutenant. If we make it through this, I just want you to know that I'm going to make your entire platoon do a strip tease for my personal enjoyment." Her tone hardened. "This is Captain Scollard of the *Renegade*. He'll show you where your men can load out."

Ojambe gave a sharp whistle and shouted out, "Third platoon! On me." A column of men and women in full combat gear double-timed it across the flight deck.

Sam eyed Addison. "What makes you so sure you can get onto the *Invincible*'s flight deck?"

"I told you, Sam. I blasted the hell out of that place as we left. There's no way Baltasar could have repaired it by now."

"That's your theory."

"That's my theory," Addison agreed.

"And what happens if the *Renegade* shows up and the blast doors are closed?"

"Then I blow them open."

"How are you—" Sam's jaw dropped. "You're flying ahead of them? Addison, that's crazy. The *Renegade* is cloaked, but you'll be a sitting duck. Girl, you've got a death wish."

Addison shook her head. "I've got it all worked out. One shape-charged missile right on the door seam will blow them right open."

"And what are you going to use for targeting? You've got no missile lock, no fire control. If you don't hit it exactly right, you'll end up like a bug on a windshield."

Addison forced a smile. "Then I'll just have to hit it right, won't I?"

***

"Ten minutes to Swarm contact," the intercom blared out on the flight deck. Laz stood on the *Renegade* loading ramp, his eyes searching the crowd of people in the hangar.

He finally spotted Addison near a trio of X-23 fighters. She seemed to be looking for someone in the crowd, too. Their eyes met; she raised her hand.

Laz fought through the scrum. Addison had redonned her flight suit, and her helmet dangled from her hand. She smiled at him—a real smile—and Laz felt his stomach drop through the floor. How many times had he dreamed about seeing that smile again? Gone was the disappointment, the hate, the mistrust, and all that was left was . . . Addie.

"I guess this is goodbye," she said.

"Listen, Commander, I need to—"

"Call me Addie, Laz."

"Really?"

She blinked and looked away. "Whatever happens today, I want you to know that I forgive you. I don't pretend to understand what happened, but I don't care anymore. It was a long time ago and I got over it—over you." She swiped at her cheeks. "That's not true, either. The truth is I never got over you. I know that makes me weak, but I don't care—"

"I love you, Addie," Laz said. "Always have, always will. I did a stupid thing, then I made it worse. Look, I cheated on a test, then lied about it, and it got all out of hand . . . I was so ashamed, Addie. I couldn't face you. I—I just ran away."

"I don't care, Laz."

"But I do. I need you to know that I never forgot about —"

Addison smirked at him. "I saw your sock drawer. I saw the picture."

He blushed, eyes locked on a welded seam in the deck.

"Pilots, to your fighters," the intercom blared. A running crewman cut between them.

"I'm going now," Addison called. More people milled around them. He reached out to her, but it was too late. He watched as she climbed into her fighter and a technician closed the canopy.

Laz's eyes were still burning as he strode onto the bridge

of the *Renegade*. He slid into the pilot's seat in time to see Addison's fighter taxi onto the runway. There was a long missile strapped underneath the body of her X-23. Mimi was watching him from the copilot's chair. "You sure about this, Laz?"

"Get off if you want to, Mimi," he snarled. "I'm sure."

Mimi focused on her panel. "Aye-aye, *sir.*"

Laz hid his annoyance by tuning into the control tower frequency. They were just clearing Addison's fighter. "Cannonball, you are released for takeoff."

Laz punched the radio. "Control, this is *Renegade*. Commander Halsey's call sign is *Cannonballs*. Plural, with an *s* on the end."

"Roger that, *Renegade*. Cannonball-zzzz. You are cleared for takeoff."

Addison's voice came over the net. "Cannonballs, away."

And she was gone.

"Cannonballs, huh?" Mimi said with a wry chuckle. "Wonder how she got that nickname."

Laz nudged the throttles, feeling the *Renegade* lift off the deck.

"Just watch her fly, Mimi. Just watch her fly."

Chapter 29

SS *Renegade* – Cargo Deck

Marine Second Lieutenant Okube Ojambe waited until his platoon had quieted down, then energized the portable hologram. A 3-D representation of the *Invincible*'s flight deck hovered over the assembled men.

"Listen up, marines. We are on special tasking today. This is the ISS *Invincible*, *Constitution*-class carrier—and she's been taken hostage by the Swarm. It's our job to get her back."

The men looked at one another. Ojambe noted that the brass's effort to keep a lid on the *Invincible*'s defection had worked.

"The Swarm has agents within the Fleet—one of the reasons why there has been such op-sec around this maneuver. I'll be honest with you: we have no idea what we're getting into. We could be fighting a handful of Swarm agents . . . or we could be up against the whole crew of the *Invincible*. We will work it out on the ground, so let's talk through the plan.

"Commander Halsey and Captain Scollard will land us on the flight deck. We will deploy by squad. Battle armor, full pressure suits, no gravity, and coming in hot." He highlighted the doors connecting the flight hangar to the larger ship. "We will secure access here, here, and here." The view expanded inside the ship and he assigned sectors to each squad.

"Listen up, marines. You will stay on bottled air until directed by me. All crew from the *Invincible* are considered hostile until proven otherwise. The Swarm may have the ability to infect healthy individuals and we're taking no chances."

The *Renegade*'s deck rolled under his feet. "That's our cue to lock it down. It's going to be a bumpy ride on the way in, people, so keep your shit together." The ship bucked again, forcing him to grab onto the table for support. "Listen up. The Swarm took one of our ships and it's our job to take it back. Are you with me, marines?"

"Oo-rah, sir!" Their shouts echoed in the cargo bay.

"That's all," Ojambe said. "Hang on to your asses. We're in for a wild ride. Dismissed."

The men dispersed into their squads, some of them laughing, some praying, and a few just staring into the distance. There'd been no time to install jump seats for the men. They clipped their belts and their gear to the cargo netting that blanketed the floor of the bay.

Ojambe took his place nearest the exit ramp and checked his weapons: pulse rifle with full charge, a brace of stun grenades, a standard-issue Ka-Bar knife, and his grandfather's Colt .45 service pistol. He slipped the ancient projectile weapon out of its holster. It gleamed deadly black in the dimness of the bay and he could smell the faint scent of gun oil.

The ship bucked so hard that his ass lifted off the deck, then slammed back down. Overhead, the yellow strobe pulsed.

All around them a droning noise permeated the air.

Ojambe gripped his helmet and punched his hand in the air. "Helmets on, marines."

"Oo-rah, sir!"

The helmet muffled the droning noise of the Swarm, but the sound had morphed into a vibration that he felt all over his body. His breathing came fast and he closed his eyes to calm his nerves.

I shall not fear, fear is the mind-killer . . .

The ship heeled over sharply. "Lieutenant Ojambe, are you there?" Scollard's voice in his ear.

"Here, Captain." His voice sounded distant over the comms circuit.

"Tell your men to strap in. It's going to get ugly from here on out."

Going to get ugly? "Aye-aye, sir."

"When the strobe turns red, that's your cue, Lieutenant."

"Yes, sir."

If we live that long, Ojambe thought.

***

ISS *Victory* – Bridge

"Comms, open a channel to the Fleet," said Captain Sean Rimaud. He steepled his fingers, mentally ticking off the ships in his head: *Constitution* and *Independence* along with their Russian counterparts the *Vladivostok*, *Brezhnev*, and *Murmansk*. A host of frigates and light cruisers were mixed in with the big boys.

He studied the main viewscreen. Christ, the Swarm ships

were huge—twice the size of the *Invincible* that now headed the alien column of ships. Rimaud was painfully aware that Captain Baltasar could hear everything he was saying to the Fleet.

The comms officer started in his chair. "Captain, we're being hailed by the *Invincible*."

"On screen."

He hadn't seen Jason Baltasar in years, but the man looked as if he hadn't aged a day. Apart from the strange light in his old friend's eyes—which could very well be Rimaud's imagination playing tricks—Baltasar looked normal.

"Sean," he said with a wolfish smile. "Of course they sent you."

"Captain Baltasar," Rimaud replied, "on behalf of the United Earth Federation and our Russian allies, I demand that you—"

"Blah, blah, blah." Baltasar waved his hands in lazy circles. "You have no idea what you're dealing with, Sean. The power . . . the beauty. You can't win, so why waste all those lives? Lives that are needed for our new masters—"

"Goodbye, Jason."

Baltasar looked puzzled and sad at the same time. "Sean, make them see the light. If need be, they will destroy—"

Rimaud made a cut-off motion to his comms officer and the screen went blank. "Open a channel to the Fleet, Comms."

He sat up straighter in his chair. "Gentlemen, you undoubtedly heard my exchange with our former colleague, Jason Baltasar. Our mission is clear: total destruction of the enemy at any cost. It's us or them. As a reminder, this net is not secure. All battle comms will be done by secure text using quantum crypto. *Victory*, out."

Rimaud focused on his breathing. The interaction with Baltasar had him rattled, which was undoubtedly his old friend's intention.

"XO, to the Fleet: 'All ships engage.'" They all had their battle assignments already. All he had to do was release them. His eyes tracked back to the alien ships that filled the viewscreen. Release them to what?

Sam Avery's voice sounded loud in the quiet of the bridge. "Message sent, sir."

Rimaud gritted his teeth. "Helm, intercept course to the *Invincible*. Full power to forward shields. Keep the nose ten degrees down, helm."

"Intercept course laid in, sir," helm replied. "Nose at ten down." He let his last response lilt up at the end like a question.

"XO, let the high jinks commence."

The rest of the bridge crew exchanged puzzled looks. Commander Avery tapped a short message into the secure text circuit.

"High jinks away, sir."

Chapter 30

Fighter X-B99 cockpit – Ahead of ISS *Victory*

The secure text scrolled across Addison's heads-up display. HIGH JINKS AWAY. She threw glances out either window to her two wingmen, Howler and Wolfman.

"We're a go, gentlemen. Form on me." She pulled away, letting her two companions take up stations on either side of her craft.

"*Renegade*, *Renegade*, this is Cannonballs. I have point, stay on my six."

In his cloaked state, Laz wouldn't respond, but she knew he was there.

The bulk of the *Victory* loomed overhead. She matched speed and tucked their little band of ships close into the hull of the huge warship. With any luck, they'd ride *Victory* all the way in.

"The Fleet's engaging," Howler called out. Addison watched the *Constitution* unleash her rail guns on the farthest Swarm ship, raising a prickle of minor explosions along the hull of the alien vessel.

In response, all of the Swarm ship deployed fighters.

"Oh my God," said Meatball. "Look at them all." Hundreds, maybe thousands of curved fighters disgorged from the Swarm ships, blacking out the stars around them.

"Eyes on the prize, people," Addison snapped. "All we care about is the *Invincible*." The hordes of enemy fighters were unnerving to say the least.

The *Constitution* was pressing her advantage on the Swarm ship. She approached at flank speed, cutting a swath through the fighters and raking the alien ship with her rail guns. A brilliant green laser shot out of the Swarm ship, leaving a line of fire across the *Constitution*'s hull. But she held together.

As the *Constitution* tried to turn for another pass, a UEF frigate took a run at the Swarm ship. The brilliant green alien laser punched through the hull of the smaller ship like it was lancing a boil, leaving a puff of fiery debris where the warship had once been.

"Holy shit! They just blew up the *Tighe*!"

"Howler, focus," Addison replied, her tone edged with authority.

The Russians were playing a different game, using two heavily armored battle cruisers to team up on one Swarm vessel. She saw a string of secondary explosions start across the alien ship. A good first strike, but the big ship was far from disabled.

The bulk of the *Invincible* drew closer. "Fighters away!" Wolfman called out as the *Victory* deployed their fleet of eighty X-23s. Next to the clouds of alien fighters, they looked horribly outnumbered. The fighters broke into four-man diamond formations, angling toward the enemy fighters. Pips of light flashed like a cloud of lightning bugs. Addison saw three Swarm fighters explode almost immediately.

The *Invincible* still had not deployed fighters. Was that a good sign? Maybe Baltasar didn't have control of the crew after all. That hope died a few seconds later when the *Invincible*'s rail guns started firing, projectiles streaking past them like little meteors. Even a minor hit from one of those and it was game over. The nose of the *Victory* dropped another few degrees to give the *Renegade* more cover from the incoming fire.

The *Victory*'s rail guns replied in kind, filling the empty space between the ships with deadly fire, any one of which could shred Addison's fighter in the blink of an eye. She guided them tighter against the protective shield of the *Victory*'s hull.

The drone of the Swarm fleet filled her headphones, making it hard to think. She checked the distance to the *Invincible*. Twelve thousand meters.

"*Victory*, *Victory*, this is High Jinks, stand by to break on my mark," Addison said. The two warships were closing at a rapid rate. "Three . . . two . . . one . . . mark!"

Addison punched the throttle, driving her fighter forward. Above her, the *Victory* ceased her rail gun fire and banked away, exposing her less-armored underside to the *Invincible*. Addison winced as explosions behind her reflected in her canopy. No matter, she had a job to do.

The Swarm fighters descended on them, heedless of the fact that they were flying through *Invincible*'s rail gun fire. She laid on her cannon, trying to cut a path through the alien fighters.

"Got two!" Wolfman called out.

"Good," she shot back, "but make sure you protect your cargo, boys." They were all carrying shaped charges called "bunker busters," designed to break through the blast doors that protected the *Invincible*'s flight deck.

On her starboard side, Howler's fighter disappeared. No fire, no debris, just snuffed out by an incoming rail gun slug from the *Invincible*.

Addison cursed. "Wolfman, take your run now!"

Her remaining wingman flashed by her toward the *Invincible*. She could see now that the huge blast doors were sealed shut, making Addison curse in a long, low, continuous stream. Her wingman streaked straight at the doors, releasing his missile at the last minute before banking away. When the explosion cleared, the blast doors were still there.

Laz's voice in her ear. "Cannonballs, this is *Renegade*. I'm hit; my cloak is down."

Addison chanced a glance over her shoulder. The *Renegade* was in full view and trailing a stream of plasma from the right side. Enemy fighters swooped in and she responded with continuous fire from her turrets.

Invincible loomed large before her. It was now or never.

"Listen, Laz. Stay tight on my six, I'm switching the missile from targeting to contact. I'm going to drive it straight in."

In her peripheral vision, she saw one of the Russian heavies explode in a massive ball of fire that was immediately snuffed out in the vacuum of space.

"Addie, pull back. We'll find another way," Laz pleaded with her.

"Nope. We're going big or going home, Laz. Stay on my six and you'll be fine."

"Addie—"

"No time," she cut him off. "Just remember what I said back there."

She switched the radio off. It was hard not to feel small next to the bulk of the *Invincible*. The blackened blast doors filled her viewscreen. She pushed the throttle all the way forward and held the trigger down in continuous cannon fire as she sped at the doors.

Addison released the missile, watching it streak ahead of her ship. She had maybe five seconds to impact.

The fiery explosion filled her viewscreen, licking out toward her.

All she could hear was her own screaming.

***

SS *Renegade* **– Bridge**

"Laz, it's suicide!" Mimi screamed. "Slow down. Let's hold off until we know if she gets through."

"She'll get through." *What are you doing, Addie? Do you have a death wish?*

Mimi stared at the hull of the *Invincible* that was getting closer and closer at a rapid rate. "How do you know?"

"She'll get through," Laz repeated. He punched the channel that patched him to the marine lieutenant in the cargo bay.

"Ojambe, this is the captain. We're on final approach to the *Invincible*. Either we're going to be a bug on a windshield in the next thirty seconds or you're going to be shooting some bad guys. Right now, it's a toss-up."

"Yes, sir."

"Don't call me sir, Ojambe. I work for a living."

The marine didn't reply.

Mimi, her face white, sat back in her seat and tugged on the straps of her harness. "Was that necessary?"

Laz watched Addison's fighter streaking toward the blast doors of the *Invincible*'s flight deck. Her trajectory never deviated. He knew she never had any intention of releasing the weapon and steering away. She would either get onto the flight deck or die trying.

A Swarm fighter crossed too close in front of them and the *Renegade* plowed right through it. Laz smiled to himself.

"You're going to kill us all, Laz," said Mimi through clenched teeth.

"She'll get through."

He saw Addison release the missile, saw it streak away, saw the fiery explosion, saw her fighter enter the ball of flame.

"She'll get through," he said again.

Then he pushed his throttles all the way to the stops.

***

SS *Renegade* – Cargo Bay

Ojambe clung to the cargo netting with both hands as the deck of the *Renegade* bucked wildly underneath him. A projectile punched through the cargo bay, depressurizing the room around them.

He keyed his mike. "Brace for impact, marines."

The ship stopped for a split second, as if a giant hand had grabbed and then lost its grip. Ojambe felt his body rush toward the bow of the ship, then fly backwards again. A moment later they slammed down hard, in gravity. The air rushed out of his lungs and he gasped for breath. The cargo bay slewed sideways like they were sliding, then ground to a halt.

The flashing strobe on the ceiling turned from yellow to red and the ramp in front of him dropped, clanging against metal. Artificial light flooded into the cargo bay.

Ojambe struggled to his knees, unhooking his belt from the cargo net. He stood. "Follow me, marines."

He plunged down the ramp and onto the flight deck of the *Invincible*.

***

ISS *Invincible* – Flight Deck

Bright light. Pain.

Addison cracked open one eyelid.

If I can feel pain, I must not be dead.

She was upside down, mashed into a corner of the flight deck, her fighter nothing more than a few shreds of metal and composite around her.

But she was alive.

Her fingers scrabbled for the buckles on her harness. Too late, she realized that the flight deck still had its artificial gravity energized. Her body crashed into the floor. More pain.

She sat up, testing her limbs one by one. Nothing broken.

The *Renegade* lay a hundred meters away, battle damage evident. The ramp dropped and armed marines flooded from the rear of the craft.

Addison struggled to her feet, limping toward the *Renegade*.

Her head was starting to clear. They'd done it. They'd gotten back on board the *Invincible*. She wanted to cry and scream at the same time.

Addison took a knee, trying to catch her breath. Every muscle ached and she had a splitting headache.

The hand from a pressure suit entered her field of view. She looked up at Laz. "Can I give you a hand?" he said over the intercom.

He hoisted Addison to her feet. "I thought you were trying to kill yourself back there."

"Hey, you know me. If it's worth doing, it's worth doing at Mach two." It even hurt to smile.

The marines had deployed across the flight deck and secured all three entrances to the ship. Maybe this wouldn't be that hard after all.

Laz smiled. "Let's go get your ship back, Addie."

Behind him, the main entrance to the flight deck erupted in a ball of fire.

Chapter 31

ISS *Victory* **– Bridge**

"Decks Four through Twelve are depressurized, sir. Lasers are offline, but rail guns are still fully functional." Sam Avery's voice was steady. Thank God for that, because the rest of the bridge crew looked like they needed a fresh change of underwear.

"What about torpedoes, XO?" Rimaud said.

Avery shook her head. "No joy, sir. We took a direct hit to the operating system. It's possible we could launch them manually, but we've lost comms with that deck."

Rimaud surveyed the battlefield.

The smaller ships were pretty much helpless against the superior firepower of the Swarm lasers. He'd watched at least eight of them get destroyed with one blast, their shields absolutely useless against that much concentrated energy. They stood a decent chance against the alien fighters, at least.

Their own fighter squadrons were able to outfly and outgun their opponents, but they were still outnumbered ten to one.

In short, it was a bloodbath out there.

The battle was going to come down to whether the heavies from the UEF and Russian fleets were able to take out the Swarm ships. And the difference-maker was the *Invincible*.

Captain Baltasar used the superior maneuverability of his vessel to make up for the slower Swarm ships, darting into one-on-one Earth-versus-Swarm matchups to throw the balance in the alien's favor.

He watched as the *Constitution* took another withering barrage of Swarm laser fire while the *Invincible* went low to rake her vulnerable underside with rail gun projectiles. Geysers of atmosphere sprouted from the *Constitution*'s belly.

Rimaud snarled to himself. "XO! What's the status of Halsey and *Renegade*? Did they get onboard the *Invincible* or not?"

"I can't tell, sir," Avery replied. "There was a huge explosion near the flight deck, but I don't know if that was them getting in or . . ." She let the rest of her thought go unsaid.

"Alright, the *Constitution* is getting slaughtered out there. Tell the *Independence* to form up on my port side and let's go after the Swarm ship. Maybe we can draw their fire off the Connie for a while."

"Aye-aye, sir," Avery shot back. "The Indy is in formation. Standing by."

Rimaud pointed to the jagged crack in the hull of the Swarm ship. "Concentrate our rail gun fire on that location. Tell the Indy to follow us with as much laser energy as they can muster."

The hull throbbed with the familiar pulse of rail guns. They were using thirty-kilo slugs, the biggest they had, on the

Swarm ships. Rimaud thought he could see the damaged area expanding. He pounded his fist on the armrest.

"Tell the Indy to finish this bastard off!" he shouted.

"The Swarm ship is returning fire, sir!" Avery called. The now-familiar green laser blasted toward them, blanking out the viewscreen.

"Direct hit, but the hull is holding," Avery said. "For now." Rimaud thanked the ship designers again for the meters of tungsten that protected them from the emptiness of space. The Swarm ship on the screen began a slow roll as explosions consumed her.

"The Swarm ship is breaking up! We did it!"

"Head in the game, people," Rimaud said. "That's one of four. What's the status of the *Constitution*?"

"*Constitution* has lost main propulsion, but she still has weapons."

"Good, where's—"

The ship pitched forward.

"The *Invincible* is on our six, sir!" Avery shouted. "She's targeting main engines!"

"Hard starboard!" Rimaud roared. He stopped in mid-command. Whatever evasive maneuver he gave, Baltasar would recognize it and counter immediately. He needed to do something completely out of the box. "Helm, all stop!"

"Sir?" The helm gaped at him.

Avery leaped past him to the helm station, stopping the engines. "All stop, sir!"

The *Invincible* screamed past them.

"Target her main engines, Weapons," Rimaud screamed. "Fire!"

The *Victory*'s rail gun fire rained down on the *Invincible*'s exposed rear, tearing into the ship's hull. A blast of plasma ejected in a bright corona. "We got a hit, sir!" shouted Avery.

Too late, Baltasar realized what had happened, and he began slewing the ship around in a tight circle. The Swarm ship's laser blazed at them, overloading the viewscreen.

"XO, message to Indy: 'You take the Swarm vessel. We've got *Invincible*.'"

"Message sent, sir."

The screen cleared and Rimaud saw the *Invincible* bearing down on them fast, rail guns and lasers blazing.

Rimaud drew in a deep breath. So that's how it was going to be. "All power to forward shields. Direct all rail gun fire on the *Invincible*'s damaged side. Intercept course to *Invincible*." He waited for the acknowledgments, then sat back in his chair. The seat throbbed with incoming and outgoing rail gun slugs.

"XO."

"Sir?"

"I've got a job for you."

Chapter 32

RSS *Murmansk* **– Bridge**

Captain Sonya Gubanov hated sitting in her command chair during a battle. She liked to be on the move. She placed a manicured hand on the helmsman's shoulder. The young man trembled under her touch. Gubanov knew how he felt. Seeing a warship like the RSS *Brezhnev* destroyed in front of you would do that to anyone.

"Easy, Comrade Androvich," she said in a low voice. "We will get through this." The lie was needed at a time like this. The Swarm ships were huge things, their fighters like clouds of wasps that stung them over and over. They would be lucky if any of them made it through the day.

Their lasers were all but ineffective on the exterior of the alien ships. But if they used projectile weapons to puncture their hide, then lasers had more of an effect—providing they could fight their way through the clouds of fighters to get within laser range.

"Get me the captain of the *Vladivostok*," Gubanov barked.

"On screen, Comrade Captain."

Captain Yelizarov was one of the old-school warship

captains. Unlike the newer political appointees, he'd clawed his way up through the ranks. The man was older, maybe mid-sixties to Gubanov's forty-five, and his lined face showed signs of hard living.

"Comrade Captain," he said, his voice flat.

Gubanov wasted no time. She was the senior Russian officer now and the battle plan was hers. "Captain Yelizarov, I'm pulling all the smaller ships back. They will work with the fighter squadrons to take out as many enemy fighters as possible. You and I will concentrate on the Swarm vessel."

Yelizarov grunted.

"Form up on my port quarter for a full-speed run. The *Murmansk* will use rail guns to open up the alien hull. I want you to concentrate laser fire into the damaged areas."

Yelizarov nodded. "I concur, Captain." He cut the comms channel.

Gubanov spun toward the helm. "Bring us out, Comrade Androvich. I want to run down the Swarm ship starboard side." She watched the helm work, then said, "Engage."

They closed the space between them and the alien ship quickly. "Weapons Officer, continuous rail gun fire. Let's see if we can open a seam in this big bastard."

"Incoming laser fire, ma'am!" The green light oversaturated the viewscreen and the ship buckled under the massive energy impact.

Gubanov swung into her command chair and buckled the seat belt. "Divert all remaining power to shields," she said.

"Shields at fifty percent and dropping, ma'am."

"Very well, Sensors. Keep firing, Weapons Officer."

The ship lurched, and she felt their speed drop off.

Gubanov stabbed at her armrest. "Engineering! Report!"

"We took a direct hit to the mains, ma'am. We've got thrusters only for now." She could hear screams and explosions in the background.

"Helm, spin us so we are facing the alien vessel. Full power to forward shields. Weapons Officer?"

"Still firing rail guns, ma'am." Gubanov could see a hole developing in the side of the alien vessel. She nodded. "Good work, Comrade Lostov."

The green laser blazed at them again. Her ship slewed under the directed energy. It wouldn't be long now.

"Engineering reports that main engines are unrecoverable, Captain," said her XO.

Gubanov nodded. She couldn't take her eyes off the burning hole they were forging in the alien ship. "XO, tell the *Vladivostok* that we're leaving them a nice opening to work with. Tell them to finish this bastard off."

"Captain, we're being hailed by the *Vladivostok*."

"On screen." The Swarm noise was deafening and the screen kept pixelating as Captain Yelizarov's face came into view.

"Captain," he said, "I'm maneuvering my ship between you and the Swarm ship. Keep up the rail gun fire. I'm going to target the damaged area with lasers."

"Captain, that's only going to get both of us killed. Get out of here—" But she was talking to an empty screen.

"The Vlad is moving in front of us, Captain!" The effect was immediate. The hull of the *Murmansk* stopped vibrating.

Gubanov stepped out of her chair. "Sensors, extend our shields around the Vlad. Divert all power to forward shields.

The only thing I want running is shields and rail guns."

"Even life support, Captain?"

"Even life support."

The *Vladivostok* poured laser fire into the opening in the Swarm hull. A billow of fiery debris started to drift from the hole.

"Incoming fighters, Captain!"

"Ignore them."

"Ma'am?"

"You heard me, comrade. Keep firing on the Swarm ship."

The Swarm laser lit the combined shields of the *Vladivostok* and the *Murmansk* a sickly green. Alien fighters crawled across the screen like ants, shooting blips of fire. Sonya felt the deck plates of the *Murmansk* rattle as the fighters found their mark on vital systems.

But she kept her focus on the Swarm ship.

A ripple started on the edges of the damaged area. Gubanov smiled. With an incandescent flash, the hide of the Swarm ship buckled under a series of secondary explosions.

The green laser stopped firing. The screen filled with fiery destruction.

"Full reverse thrusters," Gubanov said. It was a meaningless gesture. There was no way they'd be able to escape this explosion.

She looked down to see a secure text from Yelizarov scroll across her screen. *Dasvidanya, Comrade Captain*."

The Swarm ship erupted.

Chapter 33

ISS *Invincible* **– Flight Deck**

Second Lieutenant Ojambe picked himself off the ground, his ears still ringing from the explosion.

"Fall back," he yelled into his microphone. "The doors are booby-trapped. All squads, fall back!"

He waited for the reports from his squad leaders. Correction: squad leader. Two of his sergeants had been among the seven men killed in the explosion. He cursed to himself. He should have been more cautious, should have sent in bomb-hunting drones.

Scollard and Commander Halsey joined him, trailed by Topper and Little Dick. Together, they approached the blackened hole that had once been the main entrance onto the flight deck.

"Guess they figured out we were coming," Laz said.

"We need to move, Lieutenant," Addison added. "We need to get this ship back and get her in the fight."

"Yes, ma'am." Ojambe projected the 3-D image of the *Invincible*'s decks from the hologram device on his forearm. He wanted to shake his head but stopped himself. The ship was huge. It would take the better part of a day to clear, especially if they needed to search for booby traps around every corner.

He started highlighting sections. "Sergeant, you take first squad and—"

"Wait, Lieutenant," Halsey interrupted. She was studying the image and tapping her foot. Through her faceplate, Ojambe could see a trickle of dried blood on her temple. "Let's think about this. Since there's no armed force here to greet us, we can assume that Baltasar has not been able to infect the whole crew, right? So where are they?"

She pointed to a spot three decks up from their location. "These are the mess decks. Besides this hangar, that's the only place on the ship you could hold a large group of people. Let's start there."

Ojambe nodded. His finger traced a track through the ship. "So we get there by moving through—"

Halsey interrupted again. "Send a squad that way, but let's also take a group through the maintenance tubes. Maybe we can catch them by surprise."

Ojambe divided his remaining men, putting a team of twenty under the sergeant and the rest with him. Halsey led the group into the charred hallway to a maintenance panel, which the huge bald man removed for her. "Up we go," she said.

They climbed straight up through three decks to their destination. Ojambe released a mosquito drone through a ceiling vent to recon the hallway.

"Two men," he reported. "Armed and posted outside the mess decks. The doors are sealed. No sign of explosives outside, but one man does have a detonator on him."

He watched Halsey digest the information. "They could fit

most of the crew on the mess decks if they pack them in. But the detonator . . ." Her face went pale. "I bet he's rigged the windows in the mess decks. If we attack, he'll space them all."

Ojambe projected the detailed 3-D image of the deck beneath them, the light reflecting off Halsey's faceplate. He pointed to where two hallways converged directly below a maintenance access. "We need to get the detonator guy to this spot right here," he said.

"And then what?" Halsey asked.

The marine gave her a grim smile. "I'll make sure he doesn't use his detonator."

Laz wormed his way up next to Halsey. "I'll send Topper and Little Dick with the marines. They're good at diversions."

Ojambe stripped off his helmet and pressure suit, then carefully crawled through the maintenance tube to his destination. He peered through the grate down into the empty hall and unclipped the metal mesh. He flashed a thumbs-up back to Halsey.

"The lieutenant is in position," she whispered.

Ojambe felt his muscles tensing. He loosened his pistol in its holster and made sure his knife was secure. As the minutes dragged by, Ojambe did his best to control his breathing.

He tensed again as he heard the tread of running feet in the hallway below him. Two men, dressed as crewmen of the *Invincible*, took position beneath him, exactly as he'd hoped. One, armed with a pulse rifle, posted at the corner. The second man, holding a detonator, flattened against the wall behind him. He slipped the detonator into his pocket and spoke rapidly into a communicator. He whispered to the other. It looked like he was about to leave.

Ojambe lifted the grate. At the last second, the corner scraped and the armed man looked up.

Ojambe's weapon came out in one fluid motion. The discharge of the Colt in the space of the maintenance tube was deafening. A neat hole appeared in the man's forehead.

The marine was already through the hole in the ceiling, using one arm to flip his body so he landed on his feet. His weapon came up again, but detonator man lashed out with a kick that knocked the Colt away. The man backpedaled, digging in his pocket for the detonator. Ojambe lunged forward, punching the man in the throat.

Choking, the man jerked the detonator out of his pocket, mashing down the red button. Ojambe covered the man's thumb with his own and held on. He body-slammed the detonator man against the wall, driving his knee up at the same time. He felt the man's body contract in a tight spasm of pain.

Ojambe fought to keep the detonator depressed. The man thrashed under him. Ojambe head-butted his captive, then used the split second of disorientation to draw his Ka-Bar knife.

As the man made one last attempt to break free, Ojambe drove the knife into the soft flesh under the man's jaw, snapping his teeth shut with a solid click. The man with the detonator stopped moving.

Ojambe heard footsteps behind him and he turned to find his marines and Scollard's two men running down the hall. He smiled. "He depressed the dead-man switch, but I got to him first." He let the body slide to the floor, then sat down next to it, careful to keep his own thumb firmly on the dead man's thumb. "Looks like I'll be camping out here for a while."

The man they called Topper stepped forward, drawing a razor-sharp machete from a scabbard slung over his shoulder. He slashed once, severing the dead man's hand at the wrist.

He grinned down at Ojambe. "Hey, Lieutenant, looks like you're mobile again."

Chapter 34

ISS *Invincible* – Mess Decks

Addison gathered with the rest of the team outside the door to the mess decks. Ojambe was carrying a severed hand that dripped blood on the floor. The sight made her want to gag.

Laz examined the doors. "They look okay, but we have no idea what's on the other side. Shall we open them?"

Addison felt the ship bank at a hard angle and the pulse of the rail guns firing rippled through the deck plates, reminding her of the battle that still raged outside. She shook her head. "We can't risk it." She looked up. "I'm going to climb through the maintenance tubes and punch a hole through the roof."

"I'll go, ma'am," one of the marines volunteered.

Addison stopped him. "The crew knows me. When I come crashing through the ceiling it'll be easier to explain."

Quickly, she slid out of her pressure suit and found the nearest maintenance access. Laz followed her, handing her a small laser-cutting tool. "You're going to need this. Be careful, Addie."

"Always," she said with a quick smile.

Laz snorted. "Never, you mean."

Addison quickly climbed up into the main tube, then looked for a ventilation system access panel. She cut the grate off, mentally measuring the duct. It would be a tight squeeze, especially with her flight suit on. Addison stripped off her flight suit, leaving only a T-shirt and shorts.

The ship lurched heavily and lost speed. Addison winced. Her ship had just been hit.

She stretched out her arms and slid into the duct. By wriggling, she was able to make decent progress. The first vent showed light ahead of her. She peered through the louvered opening.

The space was full of crewmen from the *Invincible*, hundreds of them. Most were sitting, a few standing. Addison energized the cutting laser and sliced at the louvers. They fell into the crowd. When she looked down again, she saw faces turned up toward her.

"It's the XO!" someone said. People started milling around, talking excitedly.

"Quiet!" Addison called. "Stand back so I can make a hole big enough to get through." She slashed at the duct material until she had a large enough exit, then plunged the twelve feet down into the room. A group of the crew caught her and lifted her onto her feet.

She'd sliced her shoulder open on a jagged edge on the way through the duct. Someone started fussing with it and she waved them away.

"Where's the bomb?" she said. "We found a detonator outside. Where's the bomb?"

"Over here, XO," said a voice. The crowd parted. Addison

had been wrong. Baltasar hadn't rigged the windows to blow, he'd rigged a person. Ensign Proctor gave her a wan smile. "It's me, I'm afraid."

The rest of the crew was leaving as wide a berth as possible around the ensign. Not that it would matter. If that bomb blew, they were all dead.

Addison knelt next to Proctor. "Zoe, I need you to tell me all you can about what Baltasar's done with the ship."

She nodded. There were tearstains on her cheeks, but her red eyes were dry now. "He was able to convert the bridge crew—all except for me. I think he gave them a shot."

Addison's thoughts flashed to the test tube they'd taken from Laz's cargo. It was some kind of bioweapon that could turn humans into Swarm drones?

"Okay, what else?"

"He was working to transfer all control functions to the bridge. All weapons, all engineering, everything. He's vented all the decks between here and the bridge, too."

He's built his own little castle, Addison thought. And he's the king.

"Anything else?"

Proctor shook her head, her green eyes pleading with Addison.

"It's going to be okay, Zoe," Addison said. "I promise."

Proctor forced a smile. "I appreciate you saying that, ma'am."

Addison turned her attention to getting the crew freed. She hammered on the doors until Laz opened them. He grinned when he saw her skimpy outfit. "Do you ever stay fully dressed anymore, Addie?"

She glared at him until his smile faded. Then she spoke to the crowd. "Listen up, people. Your ship has been taken over by an alien force. Captain Baltasar is with the enemy and he's put the bridge crew under Swarm control as well. He's running the ship from the bridge." She swept her eyes across the crowd, acknowledging the nods with her own. "We need to take this ship back the hard way. Every rail gun, every laser turret, every torpedo right now is being used against our own people. I need volunteers to take back our ship deck by deck, station by station, weapon by weapon. Who's with me?"

The hands sprouted up around her.

"Crew chiefs, pick your teams and get going. Fighter pilots?"

More hands.

"Get your asses down to what's left of the flight deck and get in your birds. Every Swarm fighter you take out is one less that we have to deal with." A herd of pilots ran for the doors.

As the space emptied, Ojambe stepped forward, still holding the severed hand. "What about me, ma'am?"

Addison took Ojambe's arm and led him to Ensign Proctor. "Lieutenant, this is Zoe Proctor. You two are now roommates until we figure out a way to get that thing off her." She lowered her voice. "I don't know how to say this, Zoe, but I'd like you to move to the flight deck, just in case . . ."

Ojambe held out his hand to Proctor. "No problem, ma'am. We'll be fine."

Laz watched them leave. "Ah, young love," he said. "What about us, Addie? What are we going to do?"

Addison strode into the hallway and started to put on her pressure suit. "You and I are going to take my bridge back."

Chapter 35

ISS *Independence* – Bridge

Noah Preble, commanding officer of the ISS *Independence*, watched the unfolding battle with growing horror. The *Constitution* drifted away from the field of battle, her engines clearly out of commission. Swarm fighters clouded around her like stinging hornets.

The *Victory* had just done some kind of suicide run at the combined firepower of a Swarm ship and the *Invincible*, peeling away at the last minute and exposing her less-armored underside to devastating fire from *Invincible*. What was Rimaud thinking?

"Captain, it looks like the *Victory* was running interference for a small ship that tried to board the *Invincible*," his sensors officer said.

"Tried?"

"There was a huge explosion on the *Invincible*'s flight deck, sir. I can't tell if the ship actually made it onboard."

Preble held his face still. At least the *Victory* still had some mobility. He punched the intercom on his armrest. "CAG, this is the captain. I want you to direct your fighters to cover the

Constitution. She's out of range of the Swarm lasers, but those fighters are tearing her apart."

Commander "Ajax" Tianopolis responded immediately. "Aye-aye, sir. Redirecting now."

"Open a channel to Captain Rimaud, Comms."

The thin white face of the *Victory*'s commanding officer appeared on the viewscreen. "What's this 'high jinks' business, Sean?" Preble demanded. "You took a hell of a risk back there, sir."

"Captain!" his sensors officer broke in. "One of the Swarm vessels is breaking formation. It looks like the *Invincible* is escorting her."

Preble studied the tactical display before looking back to his fellow captain. "Sean, we're getting killed trying to take on the Swarm ships one-on-one. The Russkies teamed up and took one out all on their own." He tapped the tactical display. "While Baltasar is otherwise occupied, maybe we can do some damage. What do you say?"

Rimaud nodded. "I've lost three engines, but I've got a bay full of torpedoes. If you can drag me along with your tractor beam and open up a hole in that fat bastard over there, I can cram a whole world of hurt right down their throats."

"You got it, sir." Preble paused. "One other thing. I've sent all my fighters to cover the Connie. You might want to do the same."

Rimaud let out a hollow laugh. "That's a good idea. At least they'll have a home if . . ." His voice trailed off. "Enough talk, Preble. Let's get started. *Victory*, out."

"Captain, the *Victory* is maneuvering into our stern," his sensors officer called out.

"Very well," Preble said. "Engage the tractor beam. Ahead half speed, helm. If the tractor beam holds, increase speed." He pointed at the Swarm vessel dominating the screen. "Weapons Officer, target rail guns on that spot directly between their fighter bays."

The hull of the *Independence* stuttered under the continuous rail gun fire and the screen before them lit up with thin streaks of light. The Swarm vessel responded by disgorging even more fighters. A broad stripe of green laser fire reached out, turning the Indy's shields into a rainbow of energy.

Preble gritted his teeth. "Give em everything we've got, Weps."

Chapter 36

ISS *Victory* – Torpedo Bay

Sweat poured down Sam Avery's face. The thermal controls in her pressure suit had either failed or been overwhelmed by her exertions. Right now, she'd give almost anything to be able to wipe her face with a cold washcloth.

The thermonuclear torpedo slid into the tube, pushed by three crewmen. A fourth slammed the door shut and threw the latch. The loss of gravity in the space made the job much easier.

She felt the ship give a sudden jerk as if it was being pulled. What the heck was going on now?

"XO, what's your status?" Rimaud's voice was loud in her headset. Sam blinked away a bead of sweat that trembled on her eyelash.

"Captain, we have five of six tubes loaded. Number six in progress—give it another five minutes."

"And you've verified that you have local control to fire?"

Sam's eyes tracked over to the manual launch panel floating in space a few feet away. It was tethered to a capacitor bank. On paper, it *should* work.

"Yes, sir, we've rigged up a local launch system, but it's got some limitations."

Rimaud hesitated. "Tell me."

Sam cursed the genius engineer who had designed out the manual launch bypass on each tube that existed on the older starships.

"Basically, sir, we get one shot. Whether we fire all six or only one, the capacitor bank needs thirty minutes to charge after we use it."

"*Thirty* minutes?" Rimaud's voice was incredulous.

"Yes, sir. Thirty." Sam fantasized about putting one of those engineers in a torpedo tube and launching his ass into space.

Rimaud snapped her back to reality. "Can't be helped, XO. We're teaming up with the Indy to see if we can take out one of these alien vessels. They're towing us in and trying to open up a hole for us to dump a bunch of nukes into." Rimaud paused like he was trying to figure what to say next. "This doesn't look good, Sam. As soon as you hit the launch button, get your tail into an escape pod. Get as far away as you can as fast as you can. Understand?"

"Sir—"

"That's an order, Sam. However this ends up, UEF will need to rebuild and they'll need people like you. I'm ordering all nonessential personnel into the pods as soon as we're done here." He paused again. "You're a good officer, Sam. The best. You make sure you live to fight another day."

There was something in her eye again, but it wasn't sweat. "Aye-aye, Captain."

***

Rimaud stabbed at the buttons on his armrest. "This is the captain." He could hear his voice echoing in the distance. "With the exception of a handful of people who have already been notified, I am giving the order to abandon ship. We are about to attack a Swarm vessel with a full complement of nuclear torpedoes. Given the damage we've already sustained, it is unlikely that the *Victory* will make it safely out of the blast range in time.

"We've all lost friends and crewmates today. I don't want any false heroics, people. There's no shame in living to fight another day. May God bless you all. Rimaud, out."

He cut the feed and drew a deep breath. "Time to contact, helm."

"Six minutes, Captain." The man's voice was hoarse.

"Very well." He spun in his chair. "Comms, Sensors, Weps, I want you all to go. Mr. Welby and I have this covered from here on out."

All three started to protest and he cut them off with the flat of his palm. "Enough! You heard me—no pointless heroics. If—when—we win today, it will be at a terrible price. You are the future." He pointed at the door. "Now go."

"Four minutes to contact, sir," Welby said.

"Get the hell off my ship, all of you!" Rimaud yelled.

As the three officers ran for the exits, Captain Sean Rimaud sat down heavily. He touched the intercom. "XO, are you still there?"

"Yes, sir," she said between heavy breaths.

The ship, although sheltered from the bulk of the Swarm

attack by the *Independence*, still hummed with the drone of Swarm energy. He could see that the Indy had opened up a sizeable hole in the alien ship.

"Captain, the Indy says they are breaking in thirty seconds!" the helm called.

"Standby, Sam." The *Independence* banked away, and the *Victory* took the full brunt of the Swarm energy weapon. The screen oversaturated and Rimaud was slammed forward in his seat as the Swarm beam stopped the big ship's progress.

"Fire, Sam!"

***

Sam Avery was slammed into the bulkhead just as Captain Rimaud gave the order to fire. She mashed down the big red button.

Nothing happened.

Sam looked up in horror at the lone torpedoman she had ordered to stay behind. He was short and stocky, his pressure suit tight around his middle.

"What's wrong?" Sam screamed.

The torpedoman launched himself across the bay to where the launch panel was connected to the capacitor bank. The bank was behind a cage that was covered in warning signs. "That last hit knocked the whole bank off its base, ma'am. Let me—"

He wriggled his stout body between the capacitor bank and the wall and heaved backwards. The bank moved a few inches. "Almost there, XO." He pressed his feet against the wall and his back to the capacitor bank. "Just a tiny bit—"

There was a flash of energy and the torpedoman was

gone. At first, Sam thought the Swarm laser had reached them, then she saw chunks of exploded pressure suit. He'd shorted out the capacitor bank.

Sam hauled the launch panel to her. The indicator showed yellow—partial charge. She punched the red button and four torpedo tubes launched.

"Torpedoes away, Captain!"

Sam pushed off toward the far wall where the last escape pod remained. She kicked at the door switch as she passed into the tiny room. The pod launched immediately, sending her body bouncing around the capsule.

Sam Avery snagged a seatbelt and hauled herself into a chair. She faced the single tiny window, looping her arm under the other strap. She had just managed to get her body strapped in when the blast wave hit the tiny escape pod.

***

Rimaud could imagine the powerful Swarm laser blasting away at the meters of tungsten that sheltered him from space.

Sam! What the hell is taking so long?

"Steady, helm," he said. It looked like they were driving right into the mouth of hell.

Seconds felt like hours in the maddening drone of the Swarm energy. He could count on Sam. She would get those torpedoes on target—as long as he held on.

A huge bang sounded somewhere behind him.

"Shields are gone, sir," the helmsman shouted.

"Torpedoes away, Captain!" came Sam's voice over the intercom.

"Hard starboard, helm!" Rimaud cried. "Engineering, give me everything you have left."

The Swarm laser tracked them, cutting a heavy swath of destruction across their exposed side as they turned.

Then it stopped.

"Put the Swarm ship onscreen, Welby."

The alien vessel was expanding like an enormous fiery balloon. It exploded, and the shock wave rushed at them. *Victory* rolled, slamming Rimaud back in his chair.

"Damage report, Welby!"

"Engines are gone, shields are gone." He hammered at his console, then looked up. "Sir, we're falling."

Rimaud's head was still ringing from the knock he'd taken. "Falling? What does that mean?"

Welby pointed at the screen. Earth, blue and green and brown, wreathed in wisps of clouds, looked so peaceful from this height.

"We're caught in Earth's gravity, sir. We're going to crash."

Chapter 37

ISS *Invincible*

"What the hell did they do down here?" Lieutenant Don "Mustang" Havers asked his crew chief. Although they'd managed to restore artificial gravity and rig up a force field to keep atmosphere in the hangar, the flight deck of the *Invincible* was an unholy mess.

The older man laughed. "This is what happens when the XO gets angry, sir." He pointed to a wrecked fighter mashed against the bulkhead. "That's what's left of her fighter."

Mustang took in the shattered canopy and shreds of fuselage. "Cannonballs flew in on that?"

"Yep, right through the blast doors, I hear."

Mustang let out a low whistle as the crew chief closed his canopy. "Remind me never to piss off the XO again. Ever."

He moved his craft into the flight pattern. "Greyhound, Piledriver, Shrek, radio check."

Mustang nodded as his flight team checked in. Soft-spoken Greyhound, a tall, thin girl with a Midwestern accent, gruff Piledriver, and the twangy-voiced Shrek.

He keyed his microphone. "Alright, boys and girls of the

Blue Team, they're finally letting the best pilots in the entire galaxy into the fight, so watch out, bad guys." He paused. "All bullshit aside, guys. Stick to the basics. Fly straight, shoot straighter. With a little luck, we'll kill some bad guys and live to tell the story."

His headset crackled. "Blue Team, you are cleared for launch."

"Roger, Control, Blue Team is released." He punched his throttle all the way forward. "On me, Blues."

Mustang got a split-second view of the shattered blast doors as they blew past. Damn, the XO really had blown them open.

The open space outside the *Invincible* was littered with debris. Mustang dodged a chunk of metal with slagged edges. "Watch for space debris, guys. It's like a junkyard out here."

"Look at that," Greyhound said. "Is that the *Victory*?" A *Constitution*-class warship had entered the earth's atmosphere. The leading edge of the ship glowed with heat.

"Where's the bad guys?" asked Piledriver. "I only see one Swarm ship."

"Looks like we're whupping their asses," said Shrek.

The lone Swarm vessel, unharmed, loomed ahead of them. As they watched, the alien ship released a weapon toward the earth. North America was passing beneath them, and Mustang watched as the fiery weapon shot through the atmosphere, landing somewhere in the Midwest.

"Oh my God," said Greyhound.

"Blue Team, vector to ISS *Constitution* to provide fighter support. Incoming coordinates."

"Roger, Control." Mustang fed the new coordinates into

his system. The Connie was drifting, surrounded by dozens of Swarm–human dogfights. He swung close to the *Invincible*'s hull. Out of the corner of his eye, he saw movement—it looked like two tiny figures moving on the outside of the ship's hull.

"Hey, did you guys see that?" Mustang said.

"See what?" Shrek replied.

"It looked like someone was climbing the hull on the outside of the . . . oh, never mind," Mustang said.

***

Addison tried to pace her breathing. Sweat ran freely down her back and legs and she could feel it pooling in her magnetic boots. If they made it through this alive, she had some serious design suggestions for the pressure suit engineers.

A diamond formation of X-23 fighters flashed by them, vectored toward the *Constitution*. At least part of the *Invincible* was getting into this fight, but unless she managed to stop Baltasar, they'd all look like the Connie—or worse.

It was hard not to just stop and watch the battle around them. It looked like maybe the Fleet had finally figured out a strategy to defeat the Swarm ships. If they could penetrate the Swarm hulls with enough projectiles, the Fleet energy weapons were able to do some serious damage on the interior. Otherwise, the lasers on the Fleet ships seemed to have as much impact as shining a flashlight on the alien vessels.

The Swarm lasers, on the other hand, were fearsome things, able to punch through the weak shields on the smaller warships in only a few seconds. Only the *Constitution*-class warships with their heavily armored hulls and high-capacity shields stood a chance against that much directed energy.

But the new Fleet attack strategy came at a fearsome cost. The Connie was a floating hulk being picked apart by fighters, the Indy was still capable but wounded, and the *Victory* . . . the *Victory*—and her best friend—were hurtling through Earth's atmosphere like some giant piece of space junk. She'd seen the escape pods raining from the *Victory* before she made her final run at the Swarm ship. Hopefully, Sam was on one of those. Knowing her best friend's never-give-up attitude, Addison didn't hold out much hope.

Addison set her chin. The *Victory*'s sacrifice would not be in vain. Not if she had anything to say about it.

The combined Russian–UEF fleets had taken down three of those big alien bastards, but the last Swarm ship was unharmed. It coasted through space in front of the *Invincible* like a whale, unfazed by the sea of destruction around them. Laz tapped her on the shoulder, pointing at the Swarm ship.

A bubble of light exited the bottom of the ship, entered the atmosphere, and sped toward a spot in the middle of America.

Addison tore her eyes away from the spectacle and climbed even faster.

***

It's a common misconception by civilians that all ships of a class were built exactly the same. Not true. They were *mostly* the same, but each ship had variations. Sometimes these differences were new systems or design changes that were being phased into future builds. Usually they were minor: a few extra rivets or a larger control panel.

But sometimes they were major changes. The *Invincible* had one such change.

Most warships of the era had bridges that were exposed at the very top of the hull—some even had windows. But the control room of a *Constitution*-class warship was buried deep in the hull, under ten meters of tungsten shielding. When designers did this, they gave up a key factor: survivability of the bridge crew during an abandon ship event. The exposed bridge designs had a means of escape for the crew. Not so on the *Constitution*-class ships.

So one warship designer set out to fix that issue by building in an escape chute that allowed the bridge crew to exit the *Invincible* in an emergency. It was a narrow affair, only wide enough for one person, and curved so as to send the survivors out toward the stern of the ship like a slide in a water park.

That was her way in.

Addison angled their track to travel over the edge of the ship until she was walking upside down on the hull beneath the bridge. The earth spread out under her like some giant beautiful tableau. The Swarm weapon had detonated somewhere in the mid-Atlantic region, and the entire East Coast was obscured by the mushroom cloud. The flaming wreck that was once the *Victory* had crash-landed in the vicinity of Salt Lake City. A fresh dust cloud was forming in that region.

It took her precious minutes to find the bridge escape hatch. She turned on her helmet light to illuminate the area, kneeling to get a closer look at the access panel next to the hatch. Addison held out a hand to Laz for the wrench. Quickly, she removed the access panel cover, letting the bolts float away. She moved the switch inside to the position marked Maintenance, then jumpered the sensor so there would be no indication on the bridge that the hatch was open.

She nodded to Laz, who turned the handle on the access hatch. The door hung open, revealing a black entrance into the hull. They'd agreed there would be no comms between them on the off-chance that the bridge crew might pick them up. He made an exaggerated "after you" sweep of his hand.

The bridge escape exit was deliberately designed to be narrow, so Addison had barely enough room to crawl on her hands and knees, and she couldn't even turn around to check on Laz, but she could see his helmet light shining past her. That would have to do for now. Laz pulled the hatch shut behind them with a solid thunk.

The moisture that had collected in her boots leaked forward to cover her shins as she crawled along. The tunnel sloped upwards into the hull interior, and she had to use the narrow handholds in the wall to climb against the ship's artificial gravity. She was breathing heavily again by the time she reached the access to the bridge.

Addison closed her eyes, remembering the layout. The emergency access hatch was positioned at the rear of the bridge, adjacent to the lift and concealed behind a wall panel. The hatch opened outwards. Her plan was to unlatch it from the inside and burst into the bridge.

There was a bit more room here, enough for her to be able to look down at Laz. He smiled grimly from behind his faceplate, then gave her a thumbs-up. Reaching down, he pulled out a pulse pistol.

Addison slid her own weapon from the holster on her thigh. She swallowed hard and, using one hand, tried to turn the large blade switch that held the access hatch in place.

It wouldn't budge.

She reholstered her weapon, then used both hands on the hatch. The switch moved a few millimeters. She braced her feet against the wall and put her back into it.

With a cracking sound and a whoosh, the hatch fell inward. Bright light flooded over her. The atmosphere of the bridge rushed into the narrow tunnel, pinning her in place.

Addison rolled into the room, clumsy in her pressure suit, her right hand scrabbling for her weapon. Someone tackled her from behind, knocking her face-first onto the deck. There was a flash of laser fire behind her and she tried to buck off the person on her back.

She screamed and struggled, but it was all over in a few seconds. Lieutenant Anders, the comms officer, rolled her over and sat astride her chest. She craned her head. Lieutenant Yorke, the weapons officer, had a laser burn on his shoulder, but he also had a pistol trained on Laz.

His hands raised, Laz climbed into the room and sat down heavily next to her.

Anders pressed the button to release her faceplate. The thick glass swung up into her helmet, fresh air caressing her sweaty cheeks.

She felt Baltasar's heavy tread next to her head and his face came into view, blue eyes shining brightly.

"XO," he said. "You're just in time."

Chapter 38

ISS *Independence* – Bridge

Captain Preble watched the main viewscreen, mesmerized. The Swarm ship they had just attacked was billowing out in a ripple of secondary explosions. Beautiful, deadly.

No one cheered.

"Sensors, status of the *Victory*?" he asked. His voice sounded tinny in his own ears.

He'd just watched their sister ship tumble end over end in the blast wave of the exploding Swarm vessel like a toy in the ocean surf. The ship had shed dozens of escape pods and shuttles in her last run toward the alien vessel and these were scattered across space now.

"She's lost all propulsion, sir. Caught in Earth's gravity . . . she's going down, Captain."

He cleared his throat. By teaming up, they'd managed to take out three of the Swarm vessels, but now . . . *Independence* was the only Earth ship that stood between freedom and an alien victory.

"Weapons Officer, what's our status?"

"Rail guns are at eighty percent, Captain. Lasers are at sixty percent capability and shields at forty-seven percent."

Preble grunted. "Torpedoes?"

"None, sir."

He wanted to curse at whatever pinhead bureaucrat decided that they should not be fully armed, but it would do no good. "Engineering?"

"We've got five of six engines, sir. I'll figure out a way to give you whatever you need, Captain."

He wanted to crawl through the intercom and kiss the engineer right on the lips.

"Very well, Engineer." He paused. "Helm, intercept course to the Swarm ship. Full power. Weapons Officer, target that big bastard with all rail guns and commence firing. Whatever happens, don't stop. As soon as we're in range, you are free to use lasers as well."

"Aye-aye, sir," they replied in unison. The ship pulsed with the comforting rhythm of the rail guns.

"Sir?" It was the comms officer. "The *Invincible* is sending out an open hail. It looks like he's communicating with the president."

In his mind, he damned Jason Baltasar to the deepest, darkest pit of hell.

Out loud, he said, "On screen."

***

ISS *Invincible* – Bridge

Addison was hoisted up, dragged across the bridge, and forced to her knees in front of Baltasar's command chair.

She sat back on her haunches and bowed her head, the full realization of her defeat crushing her into submission in front of a man she'd once respected.

"Look at me, XO."

She kept her eyes on the floor.

"Addison," he said in a gentle voice. "Look at me."

She raised her gaze, resolving that no matter how bad it got, whatever happened, she would not give him the satisfaction of seeing her break. She would not cry, she would not beg, she would not help him destroy the only home she'd ever known.

He looked the same . . . and yet not the same. His eyes, she decided; they burned with a brightness that unnerved her.

"They are coming," he said.

"Who?" she replied, her voice sounding hollow in her helmet.

"It doesn't have to be like this," he said, ignoring her question. "They are a peaceful race, benevolent rulers. I know. I've been with them, been one of them, since birth."

"You're a spy then?"

Baltasar smiled and shook his head. "Not a spy, a messenger. We came to show you that violence is not the answer. Accept us as friends," he said with sudden sincerity. "You will not regret it."

"I think she already regrets not stopping you when she had the chance," Laz replied from his kneeling position next to her.

"*You.*" Baltasar swung on Laz. "If it wasn't for you, I would have used the Gift to change Addison, to show her the light of freedom. You ruined all that." His lip curled in disgust. "I should kill you now, but the masters accept all, even worthless vessels like yourself."

"What do you want with me?" Addison said.

Baltasar blinked. "To stop the killing, of course. I want you to tell them to lay down their weapons and submit."

"Never," she hissed.

"You cannot win. We are just the first wave, Addison. We will kill as many as necessary to achieve unity."

A chill swept up her spine. There were more coming?

Her former captain nodded at the comms officer. "Open a hail to the President. Let's see if we can talk some reason into the man."

President Quentin Chamberlain's head and shoulders filled the screen. The dark circles under his eyes showed the strain her commander in chief was under.

"Greetings, Mr. President," Baltasar said. "I have someone I want you to meet." He forced Addison to face the screen. "Allow me to introduce Commander Addison Halsey, formerly Executive Officer of the ISS *Invincible*, and now my prisoner.

"Your pathetic resistance is over, Mr. President. Your Fleet is in ruins; we have leveled two of your cities as well as more around the world. We are prepared to destroy as many as needed to ensure your compliance. You will notice the Chinese have not responded to your call to arms. That's because their leaders have already seen the light." Baltasar allowed a dramatic pause.

"This is where you surrender, Mr. President," he prompted.

"Go to hell," said Chamberlain.

Baltasar sighed. "This resistance is tiring, sir. I have told my friends to target San Francisco this time."

"Captain," said the sensors officer. "The *Independence* is approaching at full speed. She's firing on the mother ship."

Baltasar's tone hardened. "Intercept course to the *Independence*, helm. Weapons Officer, fire as soon as we are in range." He turned his attention back to the screen. "I'll be in touch as soon as I finish destroying what's left of your Fleet, Mr. President." He cut the channel.

Addison's eyes drifted to Laz. His gaze was unfocused and his lips moved as if he was counting to himself. He caught her eye and smiled.

"Take a deep breath," he whispered.

From deep in the hull under her knees, Addison felt a thump. Her ears popped and the breath was sucked out of her lungs.

Chapter 39

ISS *Invincible* **– Bridge**

Addison's faceplate snapped shut and her lungs filled with the dry, ozone-tainted air from her pressure suit. Laz had one arm wrapped around the base of the command chair and the other clamped around her waist.

"Are you okay, Addie?" Laz's voice in her ears was the most beautiful thing she'd ever heard.

"What happened?" she gasped. She struggled to her feet. The vented bridge was eerily empty; Baltasar and his people had been sucked into space.

"I put a small explosive on the outer door hatch," Laz said. "Five-minute timer."

"You didn't tell me?"

"Hey, I'm trying to keep things fresh—"

"Enough," Addison said. "Do you remember how to drive a starship?"

Laz slid into the helmsman's chair.

Addison patched her suit comms channel into the ship's system. "*Independence*, this is Commander Addison Halsey. I've taken control of the *Invincible*." She raced to the weapons station, shutting down the rail gun fire.

"*Invincible*, identify yourself."

They think it's a trick, she thought.

"Captain Preble, this is Addison Halsey. I boarded the *Invincible* and took control of the ship. I'm on your side, sir." She found the circuit to put him on screen. When Preble saw the bridge, his narrowed eyes widened at the sight of her in a pressure suit.

"Jesus, Halsey, what the hell happened over there?"

"We vented the bridge to space, sir. Baltasar and his people are gone. The *Invincible*'s back in friendly hands."

"There's one Swarm ship left and we could sure use some help, *Captain* Halsey."

Addison tamped down the rush of pride that rose in her throat. "I'm at your disposal, sir."

"Please tell me you have nuclear torpedoes."

"Full complement, sir."

Preble smiled. "Then follow me, Captain. I'll make a hole and you stuff it full of torpedoes."

The *Independence* flashed by them at full speed. Addison called to Laz, "Follow that ship, helm."

"Helm, aye," came the only slightly sarcastic reply.

The Swarm vessel loomed large on the viewscreen, a bright spot forming where the concentrated projectile fire from the Indy was opening a hole in the alien vessel. The Swarm laser blazed bright green across space, causing the Indy's shields to flare. Suddenly, the shields overloaded and the green light bored into the ship's hull. Flecks of molten slag rained into space.

"Get out of there, *Independence*," Addison shouted into the comms channel. "We've got this."

As the lead ship tried to turn away, the Swarm energy weapon raked across her flank, leaving a stripe of debris in its wake.

"Put us between the Indy and that laser, Laz!"

The *Invincible* jumped forward, the entire ship lurching as the shields absorbed the massive dose of energy from the alien weapon. Addison gripped the edge of the weapons station to steady herself as she directed their rail gun fire on the tiny opening that the *Independence* had started.

"Steady on course, Helm," she said.

The hole widened, leaving a dark gap in the alien ship's armor. She aimed her own lasers into the hole. The gap grew at a painfully slow rate.

"Addie, fire the torpedoes! We're going to run into it!" Laz shouted.

She gritted her teeth. "Just a little bit more . . ." Her finger hovered over the button to release the nuclear torpedoes.

The jagged edges of the hole glowed brightly, crumbling slowly.

She touched the button and the ship pulsed slightly as the torpedoes sped away.

"Torpedoes away! Get us out of here, Laz."

The ship banked heavily, and their side shields flared under the new strain. She checked the readout. Thirty-seven percent and dropping rapidly.

The *Independence* came into view on the screen, trailing a plume of plasma and debris, barely making headway.

Behind them, the alien laser stopped and the ship's skin began to buckle. "She's going to blow, Addie," Laz said, his voice rising.

"Wait," Addison yelled back. She engaged the tractor beam on the *Independence*. "Bring up your speed slowly, Laz. I'm going to see if we can tow the Indy to safety."

"Addie . . ."

"Do it!"

The *Invincible*'s engines strained under the combined mass of two ships.

"The tractor beam is holding! More power, Laz."

The Swarm ship started to fold in on itself, exposing a fiery core. A brilliant flash filled the screen.

"Punch it, Laz!" She stabbed at the intercom button. "All hands brace for impact!"

The deck tilted up as the blast wave from the exploding Swarm ship enveloped them.

Chapter 40

Beijing, China

Deputy Assistant Undersecretary of Off-World Aquaculture Li Zan's communicator buzzed. Not his regular work communicator, and not the communicator he used for his other job as an agent for State Security, but the *other* one.

He stared at the device. It had been over a year since his Russian handler had called him.

It rang again.

Li Zan stepped to the corner of his office and activated the localized jamming device to prevent any unintended eavesdroppers.

"*Da?*" he said in Russian.

"I have a job for you. Pickup site Omega."

The line went dead.

Li Zan dropped the communicator into the shredder and walked out of his office. His assistant barely looked up. She suspected her boss was a member of the dreaded Chinese State Security and was happy to pretend otherwise.

At street level, Zan proceeded on foot. He activated the device in his jacket breast pocket to scramble his personal signature against overhead surveillance. Probably not necessary, but better safe than sorry.

He took his time making sure that he was not being followed. Cautious agents enjoy retirement, that's what his mentor liked to say.

Zan strode into the dim sum restaurant exactly on schedule, never even pausing as he passed through the double door in the back of the room. At the rear of the kitchen, a tiny Chinese woman unloaded a wicker basket of dumplings from the steamer. She held out a covered basket. Zan accepted it and kept walking right out the back.

Outside the day was fading into dusk as he strode down the center of the deserted alley. He removed the cover of the basket to find a new communicator, a black chip the size of the nail on his pinky finger, and a picture.

Zan stopped short when he saw the picture. Even as the image began to curl when exposed to the open air, he stared.

When the image disappeared into a crumble of ash, he dropped the now-empty basket into a trash bin and started walking again.

***

It was full dark by the time Zan walked past the line of cars waiting outside Party Headquarters in downtown Beijing. He ignored the line of drivers waiting for their charges, proceeding to the elevator that led to the rooftop where the true VIPs met their vehicles.

There were only three cars here. Big, black, heavily armored craft bulging with hidden weapons and countermeasures. Zan strode to the center vehicle, flashing the wrist tattoo that identified him as a colonel in the State Security office.

"I was sent to replace you," he said.

The man shrugged. You didn't question orders from a superior officer in the State Security. Not if you wanted to enjoy retirement.

Zan slid into the cockpit of the limousine to familiarize himself with the controls. His fingers found the zip gun under the seat. All was in order.

He focused on his breathing, slipping into a state of calm. It was a job, nothing more. Just another man. His was not to question why, just to follow orders.

Three men emerged from the building, silhouetted momentarily in the square of light, then just walking shadows. Zan emerged from the cockpit and waited by the open rear door. He bowed low as the shadow stepped into the pool of light around the limousine.

Chinese Premier Sun Wu was shorter than he'd imagined, but with a youthful face and quickness of step that seemed out of place for a man of his age. He stopped when he saw Zan.

"Where's Ping?"

"Reassigned, sir. I am Zan, your new driver." He exposed his wrist to the premier. The man raised his eyebrows at Zan's rank.

"A colonel?" His gaze sought Zan's face, his dark eyes searching. "A new threat? Why was I not told?"

Zan kept his face impassive. "I believe they will be briefing you this evening, sir."

The premier grunted, then stepped into the back of the

limousine.

Zan lifted off smoothly, the lights of Beijing rolling out under them like a carpet of stars. A new dust storm was forming on the horizon, a tall stack of dirty clouds rolling in from the Mongolian desert.

He kept to the higher traffic patterns, the ones reserved for official vehicles and heavily patrolled by the military. After only a few minutes, Zan let the speed decay and he began a lazy spiral down to the premier's residence.

It was a beautiful property from above, with gardens surrounding the residence laid out in a pattern of concentric circles. He touched down in the designated space without so much as a bump and leaped from the cockpit. The tiny chip he'd been given hours before hung on the end of his index finger.

"Allow me, sir," Zan said as he opened the rear door. The premier handed out his briefcase, which Zan accepted. As the man stepped out and stretched, Zan slipped the tiny disk under the collar of his suit jacket.

"Thank you," the premier said as Zan handed over his attaché case.

Zan bowed. "It is my distinct pleasure, sir."

The premier marched into his residence.

Zan watched him go, then slid back into the cockpit of the limousine. He lifted off quickly, angling the flight path upwards but avoiding the traffic lanes. Instead, he put the craft into a long holding pattern and slipped the new communicator out of his hip pocket.

The chip he'd placed on the premier's back was giving off a strong signal. He pushed the send button.

The missile strike landed precisely in the center of the concentric circles around the Chinese Premier's residence.

Zan pointed the limousine east and pushed the throttles all the way forward. He'd be in Russian airspace in less than two hours.

Chapter 41

ISS *Invincible* **– Bridge**

Addison breathed. Not the recycled ozone-tainted air of her pressure suit but actual atmosphere.

"Wake up, sleeping beauty." Laz's voice, mocking but with a tinge of concern.

She stirred, but her eyelids refused to open.

"Hey, Addie, if you don't wake up in the next three seconds, I'm going to send your ass to sick bay."

That did it.

The bridge of the *Invincible* was brightly lit and full of people. Laz had sealed the emergency exit hatch shut and restored power to the lift.

"How long was I out?"

He shrugged. "Fifteen minutes or so." He grinned at her. "That'll teach you to wear your seat belt. Although I have to say it was pretty impressive to see you bounce off the ceiling . . ."

"Shut up!"

A technician approached Laz, who pointed toward the comms panel. "Get me a live channel to the Indy, specialist."

The man nodded and left.

Laz turned back to her. "You took a pretty good knock on the head there. You okay?"

Addison nodded. "The Swarm are gone?"

"Space dust—along with most of our fleet."

The comms specialist called out, "Sir, I've got the *Independence* hailing us."

Laz pulled Addison to her feet. She wobbled but managed to stay upright. He nodded at the comms tech. "On screen, specialist."

Captain Preble of the *Independence* looked worn but happy.

"I'm glad to see you in one piece, Captain Preble," Addison said.

"Thanks to you, Commander." He paused. "That was some fine piloting you pulled off back there . . . without your quick thinking, we wouldn't be talking right now."

Addison blushed and a sour reek pushed up from inside her pressure suit. "Thank you for saying that, sir, but—"

"Ma'am!" The sensors tech was kneeling in front of the station, the panel open at his feet. He was staring at the panel readouts.

Addison smiled at Preble. "Excuse me, sir." To the technician: "What is it?"

Laz had arrived at the panel and was tapping the screen. "Chinese warships inbound, Addie—I mean, Captain. Looks like four of them."

"Are you seeing this, Captain Preble?"

Preble shook his head. "We're completely blind for now."

"What about weapons?"

Preble winced. "I've got half my rail guns in a ready status.

Lasers are out, and I've got one engine working. We're not going to be much help."

Addison spun and took a seat in her command chair. "Yeah, well, they don't know that, sir. Use your thrusters to face them and I'll come up on your port side. Let's see if we can talk our way out of this. *Invincible*, out."

She spun in her chair. "What's our weapons status, Laz?"

"Rail guns at sixty percent, lasers at thirty, shields at twenty-five percent. Engineering reports three engines online and they're working on getting us a fourth."

Addison nodded. "Helm, take station on the port side of the Indy. If the firing starts, extend our shields around both ships."

"Aye-aye, ma'am."

"Laz, why don't you put our guests on screen and tell us who we're dealing with."

"Yes, ma'am," Laz replied without a trace of sarcasm. The Chinese warships appeared on the main viewscreen. "We have the frigates *Han* and *Ming*, lightly armored, minimal firepower. The destroyer is the ironically named *Confucius*, armed with ten-kilo rail guns and lasers. The battle cruiser is the *Zheng He*, heavy armor, twenty-kilo rail guns, high-power lasers, and a full range of torpedo options."

Addison squinted at the screen. She had a raging headache and the pressure suit was like wearing a wet towel. The Chinese vessels were unnervingly beautiful, as if the intricate designs that masked the armor somehow made them more deadly. If either the Indy or the *Invincible* were at full strength, this wouldn't even be a contest, but in their present damaged state . . .

Addison touched the intercom on her armrest. "CAG, this is the captain. I want you to muster every fighter you have. I don't care if they have no weapons or they're just trainers. If it flies, get it out there."

"Yes, ma'am."

Addison waited until the fighters started to show up on the screen. "Let's see how good their sensors are," she said. "Comms, hail the *Zheng He*."

"On screen, ma'am."

The commanding officer of the Chinese battle cruiser was an elegant woman with red-painted nails and her dark hair gathered into a twist at the nape of her slender neck. Addison wondered what kind of impression she made with her battered pressure suit, sweat-soaked hair, and bruised temple.

"This is Commander Addison Halsey of the ISS *Invincible*," she said.

The woman inclined her head. "Commander, I am Captain Lao Shi. On behalf of the Chinese Intersolar Republic, I demand your surrender."

The bridge of the *Invincible* went taut with silence. So much for small talk . . .

"I beg your pardon," Addison replied.

"The Chinese government has reached an accord with the alien race, the ones you call the Swarm. We will accept your surrender on their behalf."

"I'm sorry to disappoint you, Captain Lao," said Addison, trying to control her rising anger, "but all of the Swarm ships were destroyed. No thanks to you."

The Chinese woman smiled. "More are coming, Commander Halsey. Your choice now is to surrender or be destroyed."

Addison tried to think of a worthy response that didn't involve swearing or name-calling. Nothing. She signaled to cut the feed. The screen switched to show Captain Preble's head and shoulders.

"It sounds like diplomacy is not an option, Captain Halsey. I think we've got one more fight on our hands." Preble sounded weary and bitter at the same time.

Addison ignored her battlefield promotion to commanding officer. "Captain, I propose we link our tractor beams together and fight with our two ships as one unit. Agreed?"

Preble nodded. "Unorthodox, but it makes the best of a bad situation. We'll be stronger as one."

Addison looked over at Laz. "I'm on it, ma'am," he said. The ship rocked as the tractor beams connected.

She touched the intercom. "CAG, your fighters are our only edge in this battle. I want you to concentrate everything you've got on that destroyer. Ignore the frigates for now." She smiled to herself. "Captain Preble and I will handle the big bastard."

"Ma'am, I'm showing the Chinese fleet powering up weapons."

She caught Laz's eye. He winked at her and she smiled back.

Bring it on.

Chapter 42

White House, Washington, DC – Situation Room

President Quentin Chamberlain watched Russian President Ivanov's face as he was ushered into the White House Situation Room. The heavy lids twitched up slightly as he took in the scene.

"I thought it would be bigger," he said in his thick accent. "Ours is bigger."

Chamberlain indicated an open chair at his right hand, where the vice president normally sat. "Please, Oleksiy, sit here, next to me." He wanted to scream at the Russian to hurry up but kept a patient smile fixed on his lips.

Ivanov took an attaché case from his aide—undoubtedly a spy. He drew out a hologram device and showed them an infrared view of an aerial nighttime scene. Chamberlain could just make out what looked like an estate or maybe an arboretum.

"This is the private residence of Chinese Premier Sun Wu. One hour ago," said Ivanov. A blaze of light flashed across the screen and the arboretum exploded in a fireball. "We had confirmation that the Premier was a Swarm agent. He has been terminated."

The secretary of state was making choking noises. "Mr. President, this is a massive violation of international law. An— an assassination . . ."

Chamberlain glared at her. "Thank you for your input, Kathy, but I'm afraid this issue transcends our national borders. We are talking about an existential threat." He nodded at Fleet Admiral Kilgore.

"Two hours ago, the Chinese fleet sortied four warships to meet what is left of the UEF forces," the admiral said. "I'm afraid we have only two partially capable *Constitution*-class warships left and they are not a match for the incoming Chinese."

"Thank you, Admiral," Chamberlain said. "Winston, what do we know about these Swarm agents?"

The Director of the CIA threw an uneasy look at the Russians. "It's alright, Winston," Chamberlain assured him. "We are working with our Russian friends on this issue."

Winston Huxley sighed. "Yes, sir. Our preliminary analysis indicates that all of the Swarm agents we've uncovered to date have only two common traits. They are all roughly the same age—early forties—and they were all orphans. That's very preliminary, sir, based on the few cases we've uncovered."

"How many confirmed agents have you found, Mr. Director?" Ivanov asked.

Huxley waited for the president's nod before he answered. "Six, including the Chinese premier."

Admiral Kilgore interrupted. "Mr. President, we have word that the Chinese fleet has made contact with the *Independence* and the *Invincible*. They have demanded their surrender."

Chamberlain shot a look at Ivanov. "Satisfied, Oleksiy?"

The Russian nodded.

Chamberlain sat up in his chair. "Get the Chinese Politburo. Keep the view tight on me."

A few seconds later, the screen showed a long table with four men and two women. A thin Chinese man with a gray fringe of hair sat at the end of the table. There was an empty seat next to him.

"President Chamberlain," the man wheezed.

"Minister," Chamberlain said. "I expected to speak with Premier Sun. Is he available?"

"Our premier has been detained. Perhaps I can help you?"

Chamberlain's tone took on a hard edge. "Yes, you can, Minister. You have four warships in orbit demanding the surrender of a UEF vessel. Perhaps you can explain?"

A ripple of glances passed around the Politburo table. "I'm sure there is some mistake—"

"There is no mistake, Minister. You will recall the warships immediately or you will suffer the consequences."

The Chinese man bristled. "You dare threaten me—"

"Your premier is—was—a Swarm agent. He has used your military to prepare for an alien invasion." Chamberlain nodded to the comms tech to widen the screen so the Politburo could see Russian President Oleksiy Ivanov sitting next to him.

"If you do not recall your warships immediately, you will be invaded from the east by Russian forces. Do I make myself clear?"

The Chinese screen froze as they put him on mute. Chamberlain tapped his index finger on the tabletop.

The Chinese Politburo screen unfroze. "Mr. President, we

are unable to comply with your request."

Chamberlain gritted his teeth. "Very well, then you will suffer—"

"You misunderstand me, sir. We want to comply, but the captain of the *Zheng He* has broken off communications with her military command structure." The man hung his head. "We have reason to believe she is a Swarm agent also."

Chapter 43

Blue Team Fighter Squad
Outside the ISS *Invincible*

"They're almost too purdy to shoot." Shrek's down-home twang sounded out of place on the fighter net.

"Knock it off, Shrek," Mustang said. His team had flown well today, but there were many, many comrades who'd been erased from existence in the past few hours. He was having a tough time dealing with that fact.

"C'mon, Mustang," came Greyhound's soothing voice. "He didn't mean anything by it."

"Sorry, guys," Mustang said. "It's been a long one."

That was an understatement. They'd barely landed back on the *Invincible*—minus a third of their squadron—before they'd been scrambled again. For the Chinese this time.

The Chinese ships *were* beautiful, although he wouldn't have any trouble shooting them up. The big battle cruiser had a dragon's head worked into the armor on the bow. As they moved in orbit, the incoming solar radiation turned the dragon's scales different colors, making it seem like the beast was moving—watching them. Pretty creepy stuff.

He twisted in his seat. The *Invincible* and the Indy were a mess. Both ships had wide swaths of melted metal on their hulls and more than a few decks vented to space. He'd only seen the Indy using her thrusters, making him wonder if she even had any of her main engines available.

As he watched the two vessels moved even closer to each other, too close by his measure. What the heck were they doing? He saw the telltale distortion of a tractor beam between them. They were linking their tractor beams?

The flat voice of the CAG cut in on his thoughts. "All fighters, this is Control. It appears our negotiations with the Chinese have broken down and this is going to turn hot. If we are fired upon, you are weapons free. I repeat, if we are fired on, you are weapons free immediately. All fighters are to concentrate on the destroyer first. All teams, acknowledge."

No sooner had Mustang responded than the Chinese battle cruiser started launching rail gun slugs. The rounds streaked across space like a trail of meteors. Mustang sighed.

"Blue Team, on me!" He slammed his throttle forward.

***

ISS *Invincible* – Bridge

"We've got incoming, Captain! Rail gun projectiles." The sensors officer's voice hitched up an octave, reminding Addison that she was not working with her normal bridge crew.

"Very well, Sensors." She felt the first impacts tremble on the hull. "Helm, give me a ten-degree down attitude. Let's take those rounds on the thickest part of the armor. Weapons, return fire. Full spread, use the thirty-kilo slugs. If they want to poke the bear, then let's show them some teeth."

The ship, linked to the Indy via her tractor beams, moved sluggishly. What they lost in maneuverability, they'd have to make up for in firepower. She touched the intercom. "CAG, how're your fighters doing with that destroyer?"

She could feel the tension under the CAG's normal calm voice. "Their point defenses are good—better than our intel led us to believe—and the two frigates are a pain in my ass. We'll get the job done, ma'am, but I'm going to lose a lot of fighters."

"Can't be helped, CAG," Addison replied. "Keep me posted."

"Captain, the *Zheng He* is on the move."

Addison cursed. The Chinese captain had figured out her advantage lay in her superior maneuverability. The battle cruiser closed quickly, shifting her rail gun fire to the *Invincible*'s less-armored flanks and following it up with laser fire when she was in range.

"Return laser fire!" Addison called out. The Chinese ship's shields glowed orange but held.

Addison ignored the undercurrent of damage reports streaming into the bridge. Focus on the battle, she told herself.

"She's making another pass, Captain." The *Zheng He* swept in, unleashing another fusillade of rail gun fire and lasers. Their return fire barely scratched the Chinese ship's artistic armor.

"Incoming from the Indy, ma'am."

Captain Preble's face was grim. "Addison, I don't think this is working. As long as we're linked, I'm holding you back. This

Chinese bitch is going to cut us to pieces."

"Sir, if I cut you loose, those frigates will have a field day with you—" She stopped short. "I have an idea."

"She's making another pass, Captain."

"I hear you, Weps. Do what you can for now. Let me know when she comes at us again."

"Yes, ma'am." The weapons officer was eying her with caution. Even Laz frowned at her. Addison ignored them both as she felt the hull of the *Invincible* take another withering dose of Chinese fire.

"Captain Preble, when the *Zheng He* makes another pass, I want to reverse the tractor beams and push apart. The resulting force will put us right in her path. She'll maneuver and I want you to—"

"Spin around and take out her main engines," Preble finished for her. "It just might work."

"She's turning, Captain," called the sensors officer.

"Very well. Helm, when we push apart, I want you to put us right in her flight path, understand?"

"Yes, ma'am," said the ensign.

Addison watched the range close between them. "Full spread of rail guns, Weps. Let's make her pay. Standby to reverse tractor beam . . . standby . . . *now!*"

The bridge crew all slammed sideways as the polarity of the tractor beam reversed. The Chinese battle cruiser filled the screen, and Addison could see the beautiful dragon mosaic on the *Zheng He*'s bow rushing at them, mouth agape. The close-range rail gun fire from the *Invincible* ripped into the Chinese ship's hull, spewing fire and debris.

"Brace for impact!" Addison shouted.

The two ships collided in a crashing screech of metal, and Addison slammed forward in her chair. They spun away from the *Zheng He*.

"On screen!" Addison said. "Show me the Indy."

Captain Preble had taken full advantage of his push away from the *Invincible*, using thrusters to position himself behind the Chinese cruiser and attacking her engine room with his rail guns. A muted explosion burst out of the right rear quarter of the *Zheng He* before the more mobile ship powered away. She raked the Indy with another round of rail gun fire. A ripple of secondary explosions started on the *Independence*.

"Rail guns! Full spread! Now!" Addison shouted.

"Captain, look! The Chinese frigates are attacking the battle cruiser!" the sensors officer said.

"Hold fire," Addison replied. The two Chinese frigates were badgering the larger ship with lasers and their smaller rail guns. As she watched, the Chinese destroyer joined in.

Addison touched her intercom. "CAG, recall your fighters. Now."

"Yes, ma'am." A few seconds later the CAG came back on the line. "What's happening, Captain?"

"Damned if I know," Addison said.

The combined firepower of the three Chinese ships on their larger former colleague was having an effect. The two frigates harried the vessel from either flank while the destroyer focused fire on her engine room.

"They're going for her—" Laz started.

"Core," Addison finished for him.

The screen lit up with a massive explosion.

Chapter 44

UEF Headquarters, New York City

The vodka, chilled to perfection, slid down President Quentin Chamberlain's throat easily. A perfect way to end a perfect day.

He'd caught a glimpse of the news feeds and the media was eating up his speech. His press secretary's idea to cast him as the Great Uniter was pure genius. The UEF forces had defeated the aliens, and now, under his leadership, the nations of Earth would band together for their mutual global defense.

The Battle for Earth, as they were now calling it, had been a close-run thing, but his military had pulled it off.

The ISS *Kit Carson*, a scout ship out in the hinterlands of space, had come across another contingent of Swarm ships and reported back to Earth just in time for his speech. They'd added in actual footage from the scout ship to spice up his delivery.

God, but those Swarm ships were scary. And that interminable droning noise they made. It reminded him of ancient Scottish warriors playing bagpipes on the battlefield to put fear in their opponents.

There was a discreet knock at the door and his aide let Russian President Oleksiy Ivanov in the room.

"Oleksiy!" he embraced his new Russian friend in his best approximation of a bear hug. "So good of you to come." He waved his hand at the sideboard. "Vodka?"

The Russian's eyelids rose a few millimeters. "Of course, Quentin."

They each drank two more shots before they got down to business. Quentin's tongue felt fuzzy, but it was okay. Today was his day, dammit. He'd saved the world and he'd get drunk if he wanted to.

"How are the repairs to your Fleet going?" Oleksiy asked. He'd loosened his tie and sprawled back in the leather armchair, one leg draped over the arm. A hairy ankle poked out of his pant leg.

Quentin threw his lanky frame back in his own chair, imitating the Russian's posture. "We're making repairs to the *Constitution*, *Independence*, and *Invincible* now. The *Victory* is a total loss—that's the ship that crashed near Salt Lake City—but the *Warrior*, from the Battle of Lagrange Station, can be salvaged. That was a pleasant surprise, I tell you."

"Your shipbuilding program is active?"

Quentin swallowed another shot of vodka. "Absolutely. Congress gave me a blank check. Spend whatever you need, they said. Lagrange Station is working again, all dockyards are at one hundred percent capacity." He winked at the Russian. "We even opened a new development facility on Mars for advanced weapons systems."

"Really? Very interesting, Quentin. What about your crews? How many senior officers survived?"

"We took some losses, that's for sure. There's going to be a whole lot of battlefield promotions, but I think we're going to be okay." Stop talking, he thought. You're babbling to a man who was your sworn enemy just a few days ago.

He put the glass of vodka on the coffee table between them. "What about the Russian Fleet? How does it look on your side?"

Oleksiy grunted and polished off another shot of vodka. "There's a saying in Russia: it's never as good as it seems."

Quentin waited for the rest of it. "And?" he said finally.

Another vodka disappeared down Oleksiy's throat. "And what?"

"The rest of the saying? 'It's never as good as it seems, and it's never as bad as it seems.'"

Oleksiy shook his head slowly. "No, the saying in Russia is only the first part."

Quentin sat up in his chair. "No matter. When shall we make the announcement? I think it would be better if we did it in Moscow rather than here in New York. I think it shows more unity between us."

Oleksiy took a long time to refill his shot glass and even more to swallow its contents. "What announcement, Quentin?"

"The speech, Oleksiy! My proposal for the Integrated Defense Force—I think 'IDF' has a nice official sound to it. If we showed anything in this crisis, we showed that we are stronger together. If you lead the way, the IDF won't be just the UEF nations but *all* the nations. We can even bring in the Chinese—after we vet them, of course."

Oleksiy's leg slid off the arm of his chair. His foot hit the floor with a solid thump.

"That will never happen," he said in a loud voice. Was he drunk? Where was this coming from? "There is no way we can allow the sovereign Russian military to be subordinate to an international organization. Surely you can understand that?"

"Oleksiy, if this is a matter of command, we can establish a rotating command structure—"

"My answer is no," the Russian thundered.

"But Oleksiy, without Russia to lead the way, the IDF will be no more than renaming the UEF military."

The Russian shrugged his heavy shoulders.

Quentin sat back in his chair, trying to puzzle through the murkiness in his head. "But we worked so well together. I thought we were friends." God, he really was drunk.

"We needed each other, Quentin. It was a temporary marriage of convenience. We needed to know how far you had gotten with detecting the Swarm agents. An ingenious piece of detective work, by the way." He poured himself another shot before continuing. "We wanted your military to test the Swarm capabilities, which you did very well." A tilt of his head and another shot of vodka disappeared. "The fighting capability of your heavy carriers—very impressive. And your captains. We learned much from them, especially Halsey. Very innovative tactician." The Russian stood. "And now I must take my leave, Mr. President." He stuck out his hand.

Quentin stood, mechanically taking the proffered hand.

Oleksiy clapped him on the shoulder. "Cheer up, Quentin. Now you understand the Russian saying, right?" He bellowed a laugh and stomped out of the room.

Quentin searched his vodka-addled mind for that saying. It

was somewhere in there.

It's never as good as it seems.

Chapter 45

Lunar Base

When she'd imagined being promoted to starship captain, Addison thought it would be a magical, once-in-a-lifetime moment, the coronation of a long career.

The real thing was a slapdash affair, presided over by a very tired-looking Fleet Admiral Kilgore. The woman looked like she'd aged a decade in the past few days. Since all of their ships were in various stages of rebuilding, the ceremony was held on Lunar Base, which had been untouched by the Swarm attack. The perfect, gleaming chrome and plastic interior of the ultramodern base felt surreal after living in their own shattered ships.

She'd also imagined the day would be hers and hers alone, like a bride on her wedding day. Instead, she shared the day with Samantha Avery.

"You ready for this?" Sam whispered as they waited for the ceremony to begin.

"Do I have a choice?" Addison replied. She scanned the audience of a few hundred people. "I think we became ready when the Swarm showed up on our doorstep."

"Is he coming?" Sam asked.

Addison tried to pass it off. "Who?"

"C'mon, Addison, this is me you're talking to. Laz, of course. Is he coming?"

"I—I'm not sure."

"Do you want him to be here?"

Now, that was *the* question. Did she really want him here? Whatever they'd once had—and lost—was long gone. And now . . . there was no time for a personal life, no time to see if they could make it work. She was a warrior. Her country needed her. Hell, her world needed her.

Addison met her friend's gaze. "Honestly, I don't know if I do or not." She shook her head. "You know what? No, I don't want him here."

Sam looked at her with narrowed eyes. "For what it's worth, I was wrong about Laz. He made a mistake a long time ago, but without him neither of us would be standing here today. He was there when we needed him and that's what counts."

Thankfully, Admiral Kilgore's aide stepped to the podium, ending the conversation. Addison scanned the audience one last time, then sat down.

***

"Commander Samantha Maria Avery, front and center."

Sam left Addison's side and marched to face Fleet Admiral Kilgore. Her friend's face quivered with emotion as the admiral read the traditional change-of-command orders for Sam to report as captain of the *Avenger*, the newest *Constitution*-class starship set to come from space dock in a few days. After Kilgore placed the command pin on Sam's left breast, she broke with tradition and hugged the younger woman.

"Commander Addison Martha Halsey, front and center." Addison blushed at the use of her middle name.

Addison felt disembodied as she came to attention in front of Kilgore and snapped a salute. The admiral held her gaze for a long time before she returned the salute.

There was a long formal reading before they got to the part that Addison cared about: "By direction of the Commander in Chief, I hereby order you to report for duty as Commanding Officer of the ISS *Invincible*."

The room erupted in applause and Addison watched the admiral place the command pin on her chest. She returned the salute and then marched back to Sam's side.

And then it was over. There were no speeches by dignitaries or politicians; in fact, there were no speeches at all. The political–military bureaucracy was interested only in moving forward as fast as possible. Already the PR people were in full scrubbing mode to make sure what had actually happened on the *Invincible* never made it to the public. The Fleet hadn't lost a ship to foreign agents in over five hundred years and no one was going to admit this one.

Sam hugged her hard. "I never wanted to get command this way, but I'm glad I'm here with you," she said. "When we were just a couple of scared skinny plebes, did you ever think this day would come?"

Addison flashed back twenty years to when she and Sam, as first-year roommates at Fleet Academy, both confessed they wanted to be starship captains. The emotional detachment she'd felt all morning washed away and she hugged her friend as tightly as she could.

"Whoa, Addison," Sam said, breaking free. "You okay?"

"Yeah, I just . . . I'm glad I'm here with you, Sam."

"Excuse me, ladies. May I offer my congratulations?" Captain Preble's arm was in a sling and he looked like he hadn't slept in a week, but he was smiling all the same.

"Of course, sir," Sam said, wiping her eyes. "Sorry, we've known each other forever and it's a very emotional time for both of us."

Preble took her hand in his. "As it should be, Captain. You've both earned it." He grimaced. "Although your honeymoon period will be painfully short. Less than two months, if our intel is correct." That was the best guess analysts gave until the new Swarm fleet arrived in their solar system.

"We'll be ready, sir," Addison said.

Preble extended his hand. "I have no doubt you will, Addison. And I want you to call me Noah, both of you."

Addison smiled. "Alright then, Noah."

Preble hesitated, glancing at Sam. "Could you excuse us, Sam? Just for a moment?"

As Sam stepped away, Preble put a hand on Addison's shoulder. "I owe you my life." Preble's voice caught and he looked down. "More importantly, so does every man and woman on my ship. What you did out there . . . I've never seen anything like it, Addison. You're a natural. I want you to know, if there's anything you ever need from me—anything at all— you need only ask."

Addison blushed. "Thank you, sir—I mean, Noah. I just

did what I thought was right. I was lucky, I guess."

"Luck had nothing to do with it, Addison." He touched her arm. "Look at me hogging all your attention. Go and enjoy your day. You've earned it." He turned away, then looked back. "By the way, thanks for sending Scollard my way. I think he'll work out great as my new CAG."

Addison tried not to show the shock on her face. "Pardon, sir?"

"Laz Scollard. The admiral reinstated his commission and he approached me about being my new CAG. I put him in the simulator and he blew away the test protocols. Said you would give him a good recommendation." He frowned. "Is there a problem?"

Addison choked out a laugh. "Of course not, Noah. Laz is the best pilot I've ever worked with and he was with me every step of the way when we took back the *Invincible*." She bent her lips into a smile.

"The best man I've ever known."

Chapter 46

ISS *Invincible* – Flight Deck

Addison found him in the place she should have looked first. On her flight deck, onboard the *Renegade*.

Her flight deck. It still felt strange to realize that everything around her, every crewmember, every fighter, every deck plate, was her responsibility.

She paused at the bottom of the *Renegade*'s ramp. "Permission to come aboard?"

No answer.

She climbed the ramp. The cargo bay still had netting attached to the deck where the marines had strapped in for their landing on the *Invincible*. Addison picked her way across the bay to the open doorway into the rest of the ship. Her communicator buzzed.

"Proctor to Captain Halsey."

"Go ahead, Zoe." She smiled in spite of herself. Proctor had come out of the assault pretty well, considering she'd had a bomb strapped to her for about eight hours. Halsey had even heard that she was dating Marine Second Lieutenant Ojambe. Good for her.

"Captain, we're not able to get the correct parts for the short-range sensor array. I can jury-rig something to get us underway, but I wanted to make sure that was okay with you."

"Zoe, I want you to listen very carefully."

"Yes, ma'am?"

"You do whatever you need to do to get us underway, just make sure you update the schematics with any system changes. I trust your judgment. You don't need to ask me about every change. Got it?"

"Yes, ma'am."

Addison shut off her communicator. The rest of the ship could live without her for a half hour.

Her footsteps echoed in the empty corridor. The galley was empty, so she made her way to the bridge. A pair of feet, crossed at the ankles, were propped on the control panel.

"Want some company?" she called out.

The feet dropped abruptly and Laz's face appeared around the side of the chair. He'd shaved and was wearing a Fleet uniform.

"Addie . . . how did you find me?"

She laughed. "Process of elimination. I looked in every freaking corner of the ship until I ended up here."

He indicated the copilot seat. "Grab a chair."

She slid into the worn leather, then hugged her knees to her chest.

"I was at your ceremony, you know. Congrats. I know you've always wanted command." He grinned at her. "I'm proud of you, Addie."

"Thanks." She rested her chin on her knees, staring out over the flight deck. A row of shiny new fighters gleamed in the light. Her ship was almost back up to a full complement of eighty fighters. Pilots, on the other hand, were a different story. She reached out to touch his new uniform.

"Congrats yourself, Lieutenant."

"I guess they figured they had to do something for me after I saved the world and all." He laughed. "I asked for a billion credits but all they offered was a commission. All in all, a fair compromise, I think."

"Yeah." She let her eyes roam over the fighters again. "You could have stayed on the *Invincible*, you know."

"Could I?" he answered, eyebrows raised. Slowly, he shook his head. "I don't know if that's such a good idea, Captain."

Addison let a flash of anger show through. "You told Preble that I would give you a recommendation! Laz, you got expelled a long time ago for lying and you lied again to get your new job."

Laz threw her a look of mock horror. "You're not going to recommend me? After all we've been through?"

She laughed in spite of herself. "That's not the point, dammit."

"No, it's not." Laz's tone got serious.

Addison tore her eyes away and went back to counting fighters. She got to thirty before she said, "We could try, you know."

"That wouldn't work, Addie, and you know it."

Her vision went blurry. She swiped at her face. Laz put a hand on her shoulder. "It's just not our time, Addie." He sounded like he was choking.

"Captain Halsey, contact the bridge. Captain Halsey, contact the bridge." The public address system echoed in the vast expanse of the flight deck.

Addison sighed and stood up.

"What about the *Renegade*?" she asked, looking around the bridge.

Laz looked up at her. "I'm giving it to Topper and Little Dick—and Mimi, of course. I'm sure they'll lose it in a poker game within a few days, but they've earned it."

The loudspeaker blared again, calling her name. He stood up and held out his hand. "I guess this is goodbye, Addison. I wish you the best, really I do."

Addison stared at his hand, then stepped close to Laz and kissed him. His arm slid around her waist and the other hand cupped the back of her neck.

Twenty years slipped away in an instant. She tasted her past and her future on his tongue. The heat of his body recalled in her nights of joy and the pain of absence. Her chest swelled with love known and love lost until all she heard was the thunder of her own heartbeat.

She broke the kiss and stepped back.

"For good luck," she said. "And I told you to call me Addie."

Laz leaned back against the pilot's chair, breathing hard. He started to say something but stopped himself. Instead he smiled at her and offered a lazy salute.

"Happy hunting, Captain."

Chapter 47

An undisclosed location in Russian space

The airlock door rolled open, allowing Russian President Oleksiy Ivanov to walk stiffly down the ramp. He gritted his teeth at the soreness of his limbs. He hated space travel and the stress it put on his body. It would take him a week to recover from this trip.

"This way, sir." The doctor was a slim, red-haired woman with a quick step and no humor. All business, that one.

"We still have him sedated," she said over her shoulder as Oleksiy hobbled along behind her. She paused at a security station to allow the system to scan her biometrics. "He's been placed in a completely sealed environment with limited staff access. If they are communicating with him, we'll be able to determine how."

"Trust me, doctor, they are communicating with their agents."

She took him through three more security stations before they arrived at a room with a wall of solid glass. It was dark behind the glass and Oleksiy could see their reflections.

"Lights," the doctor said.

Brilliant illumination revealed a naked man huddled in the corner.

"Balasz Soldova," the doctor said, reading from a clipboard. "Believed to be forty-two years old, but since he is an orphan, there is no validated birth certificate. The first bona fide record we have is at twelve years old. Prior to capture, he was a colonel in the FSB."

The man looked up. He had a hangdog expression. If the aliens wanted to hide their agents in ordinary-looking people, they were doing a good job with this one.

"I want to speak to him," Oleksiy said.

The doctor nodded, waving her hand at the camera.

"Balasz, do you know who I am?" Oleksiy said.

The man nodded.

"I want to speak to your masters."

Balasz's eyes filled with tears. "I don't know what you are talking about," he said in a wailing tone.

The doctor leaned close to Oleksiy. "He's telling the truth, at least as far as we can tell. Maybe the Swarm needs to switch him on somehow?"

Oleksiy rubbed his chin and shifted his weight to ease his aching knees. "How do we do that?"

The doctor cocked an eyebrow. "We have a test protocol, but it will be unpleasant. And it might not work."

"What are the downsides to it?"

"It could kill him," the doctor said.

"Do it."

The "test protocol" involved suffocating the prisoner as they painstakingly opened each transmission band to search for any possible incoming signal. Even Oleksiy felt queasy as he watched the man's contortions. The blood vessels in his eyes ruptured, and his mouth gaped open as he tried to breathe.

When they cycled through a tiny spectrum of the meta-space band, Balasz's head snapped up and he glared at them through the glass.

"Stop!" the doctor shouted. "Leave that channel open and restore normal atmosphere to the test chamber."

Balasz climbed to his feet, breathing deeply of the returning atmosphere. His bloodshot eyes were bright. "What do you want?" he growled at Oleksiy.

"Am I speaking to the Swarm?"

Balasz nodded.

Oleksiy grinned. "I have a proposal for you."

If you loved *Invincible*, have I got a reading suggestion for you!

The SynCorp Saga, a near-future sci-fi series about the corporate takeover of our solar system is available right now. If *The Godfather* and *The Expanse* had a baby, it would be the SynCorp Saga.

Enter *The SynCorp Saga* **and step into our future.**

If you're a fan of old-school sci-fi, you may want to consider joining my **Speculative Readers Group**. Members get access to exclusive offers like deleted scenes, advance reader copies, and sales on all my titles.

For my complete reader catalog, visit my website at https://davidbruns.com/.

Printed in Great Britain
by Amazon